THE GUNMAN

Doc Beck Westerns Book 7

SARAH ELISABETH SAWYER

PROLOGUE

The inside of the saloon reeked with the stench of stale smoke, spilled beer, and tobacco spit. One could throw in the lingering scent of trail dust and horseflesh that clung to cowpokes lounging at the bar, and those at a table near the swinging doors. Cord Johnson stood holding the doors partly open as he calculated the position of every person in the room.

He didn't draw special attention, even dressed in his buckskin trousers, fringed jacket, and tan hat with its low crown and silver studded hatband.

But it was the men at the back table playing poker that he paid the most attention to.

Cord Johnson pressed through the swinging doors and closed them softly behind him. He angled toward the bar, his gaze never leaving the six men in the back corner. Four of them looked like ordinary cowpokes just wasting their month's pay.

But if Cord was right—and his instincts told him he was—it was the other two men he was after.

Cord ran his hand along the polished bar as he moved down it. The bartender came toward him, wiping a shot glass clean, but

Cord gave a low wave, eyes still on his quarry. The bartender halted, glancing between Cord and the back table.

The man settled the shot glass on the bar, rag laying over it. His eyes flicked to something under the bar.

Cord knew there would be a sawed-off shotgun there to head off trouble or break it up. But the bartender leaned forward and took note of the two ivory handled six-guns in Cord's black holsters.

The bartender took a large step back.

That threat alleviated, Cord positioned his back to the bar. He propped his palms behind him on the cool smoothness and rested one boot heel on the brass foot rail.

The card dealer faced him, but the man hadn't raised his head since Cord entered. The man didn't need to. His hat was pushed back on his forehead, giving Cord a clear view of his face. He fit the description. Hector White.

Of the two cowpokes seated on either side of the man, one caught sight of Cord's stare and leaned back slightly. He elbowed a cowpoke beside him and jutted his chin Cord's direction. The man looked over his shoulder. Another unfamiliar face.

But that set off a chain reaction around the green cloth-covered table, and Hector White looked up. He met Cord's steady gaze.

The man stopped dealing cards, his eyes darkening when he realized a challenge was coming his way. It was clear the man didn't realize who Cord was. There was little reason he should. Other than the past few months, Cord hadn't faced gunplay in fifteen years.

But Cord knew this was Hector White. And where he was, his partner was close by. Had to be the only man who hadn't looked up, his face blocked by a cowpoke's wide-brimmed hat.

Hector White, deck in one hand and loose card in the other, growled, "What are you looking at, mister?"

Cord didn't move, hands still spread on the bar to keep them cool.

"It depends. Are you partners with Buck Callaghan?"

The last man at the table jerked his head up and he leaned back in his chair to see around the wide-brimmed hat. The scar on the man's throat left no doubt that this was Smiley Jones. He never smiled.

Hector flinched, showing he recognized the name *Buck Callaghan*. But he said roughly, "I asked what you're looking at?"

"The answer depends on whether you ride with Buck Callaghan." He paused, watching the four cowpokes. When they didn't move, he added, "If you do, then I'm looking at two low-down, yellow-bellied cowards."

The four cowpokes quickly pushed away from the table, stirring dust. They scrambled back, two of them half-hiding behind the end of the bar. The other two pressed against the side wall. They sidestepped down it until they reached the swinging doors.

Cord watched all four from the corners of his eyes, but his gaze remained on Hector White and Smiley Jones, both of whom sat stock-still at the table.

When the cowpokes were clear, Cord straightened off the bar and dropped his tone to its greatest depths, the tone he used every time he faced death.

"Where is my sister?"

A full three seconds ticked away. Then Hector White dropped the deck of cards.

Cord ignored him as his right hand flashed down to one of his ivory handles. He drew and cocked the six-gun before Hector was on his feet.

But Cord's first bullet was for Smiley Jones. The man hadn't attempted to stand.

While the cowpokes were clearing away, Smiley had palmed a small pistol from his belt and had it aimed at Cord before Hector's deck of cards hit the table.

But today, Cord's draw was faster; his aim truer. His bullet struck Smiley in the heart, killing him instantly.

There was no other end for a man like that. At least, that was something Cord once believed.

Hector's gun was out but Cord had time to shoot him in the forearm, causing Hector to twist back over his chair. When he came around again, he held a gun in his left hand. Cord fired again, knocking Hector back into the wall.

Smiley Jones was still in his chair, body slumped over the card table, his face turned forever away from Cord. He would just as soon have it that way.

Smoking gun in hand, Cord approached Hector. The man slid down the wall, his two useless arms dangling at his sides. He was bleeding bad.

Behind Cord, the bartender shouted for someone to get the sheriff and doctor.

Cord holstered his gun. There wasn't much time. He squatted in front of Hector Smith, who was seated awkwardly against the wall, gulping air.

Cord rested his hands on his own knees, squeezing tight to keep from strangling this man.

"I asked you a question, Hector. Where's my sister? Where's Ella?"

Precious seconds went by, seconds in which Hector might die or for the sheriff to come and prevent Cord from finding the answer he'd spent the last four weeks, two days, and nine hours searching for.

Hector drew in a raspy breath. "She...ran off. Couple of days ago. Plumb...loco."

Cord's hands thrust out and grabbed the man's collar. He twisted hard.

Hector gasped, his words coming out as a gurgle. "She just... cooked for us, is all. I swear."

Cord hardly recognized his own voice when he said, long and slow, "Where...is...my...sister?"

Hector's eyelids fluttered, eyes going sightless.

"She just...cooked. She was...a good cook."

CHAPTER 1

Any day of the week, Rebekah would choose to travel by train versus stagecoach.

The stagecoach she rode in now was like trying to sit a wild bronc, the thinly cushioned leather seat not much better than a saddle. Though if Jimmy were with her, he might argue differently after having tamed so many horses recently for Doctor McKinnon.

But when the coach nearly bounced her to the floor, she doubted it. The stagecoach driver whipped up the team like a band of outlaws were chasing them.

At least Rebekah had the rocking coach to herself for the last leg of her trip. She was nearly to the town of Defiant Plains, Colorado, where she was, sadly, to escort a woman to an insane asylum.

Defiant Plains was off the beaten path with no railroad depot within sixty miles. Rebekah felt every single one of those miles as the stagecoach bounced over the rough western road. She didn't relish the return trip to the train depot in Denver, but at least once they were there, it was a smoother train ride to Pueblo—and the Colorado State Insane Asylum.

The stagecoach lurched through a mighty gully. Her hat was pinned, yet Rebekah felt it slipping to the side. She held it in place with one hand while she gripped the open window of the stagecoach with the other to keep herself seated.

Rebekah couldn't imagine dragging a poor, deranged woman across this desolate stretch by stage. Perhaps it would serve both their interests to rent a buggy and make the trip themselves.

After all, she was Omaha; the upstream people. Going against the current was in her blood.

But this patch in the Rocky Mountains was known for its unsavory characters. Two women alone in a buggy would definitely go against her uncle Robert's admonishment before Rebekah departed McKinnon Ranch:

"Whatever you do, stay out of trouble."

So far, Rebekah had managed to heed his wise words. She'd boarded the train in Centennial Ridge, Wyoming, traveled a hundred and thirty miles to Denver, and boarded the stage she now rode to Defiant Plains—all without a speck of trouble.

But then, her trip was only beginning.

Teasing aside, Doctor McKinnon's words held so much truth for her life. She needed to avoid trouble and prepare for her upcoming meeting—which equated to a trial in her circumstances—with Senator Jeffrey Harris of Wyoming, and the governor of Nebraska.

They wanted to hear her story in person: Why she was sent away from the Omaha Indian Reservation as one of only two medical doctors serving more than a thousand people. The politicians needed to know which reputation was true—that she was an exemplary medical doctor, or that she was reckless and had caused the deaths of Indian Agent Roger Graham's wife and daughter.

Sometimes Rebekah questioned her decisions of that cold, lonely night. Yet she always came to the same conclusion, and needed to share it with whoever would listen.

Traveling to Colorado to escort a woman to an asylum didn't exactly fit Rebekah's plans, but Doctor Gleeson of Defiant Plains had wired the McKinnon Ranch, specifically asking for her. He wanted a female doctor or nurse to escort this unknown woman. Rebekah would never turn down a patient who needed her.

Of course, Just Jimmy offered to come with her, but Rebekah was too pleased with seeing him settled in his place among the McKinnon ranch hands. He needed to stay and work.

Besides, this was not her first time to take a medical mission on her own.

The stagecoach lurched again and Rebekah planted her feet firmly on the floorboard to maintain her seat. Recovered, she peered out the window, relieved to see the silhouette of a town on the horizon. The mighty snow-capped Rockies towered above it, dwarfing the vision of civilization.

A short time later, the stage mercifully slowed, then came to a stop on the main street in front of a hotel. Perhaps she had time to check into a room and refresh herself before meeting with her new patient. They could both rest before the return trip.

But when the driver tossed her carpetbag to the porch where it landed with a dusty *thump*, a slim, knifelike man approached, sporting a United States Marshal badge on his vest. He stood on the boardwalk by the coach, waiting for Rebekah to disembark.

Holding tight to her medical bag, she managed the coach steps without assistance, since the marshal didn't offer any. Most men kindly wanted to carry her medical bag for her, but this marshal didn't offer to do that, either. Nor did he take his hat off when he greeted her. Instead, he offered a chilling smile.

"Are you Doc Beck, the lady doctor come to take away the crazy woman? I'm United States Marshal Hastings."

Rebekah forewent thanking the driver for carelessly tossing her carpetbag overboard as she straightened the short jacket on her navy blue traveling suit. She peered up at the marshal, who still stood on the boardwalk.

"I am Doctor Rebekah LaRoche. As to whether or not this woman is crazy, why don't you leave that determination up to me?"

Rebekah wasn't sure why her words came out so clipped. But she didn't like this man, and she had learned long ago to yield to her gut instincts, and her instincts urged her now not to trust this man.

Marshal Hastings' smile faded, but he tipped his hat to her and picked up her carpetbag. "Your patient is down at the town marshal's house. Wilde and his missus will be glad to get rid of her."

Since Rebekah only had to trust Hastings as far as the end of the street, she followed him to the pathway of Marshal Wilde's two-story clapboard house. Once on the porch, Marshal Hastings gave two hard raps on the door.

An older woman with graying hair and a pinch face answered. She gave them a stiff nod. "Is this the doctor?"

Rebekah gave a polite nod to the woman. "I'm Doctor LaRoche. Doctor Gleeson sent for me."

"Thank goodness." Her voice trembled from fatigue rather than age. "I'm Mrs. Wilde. It's a blessed relief to have you take her. She hasn't spoken a word since two boys found her wandering the dry creek bed outside of town."

Rebekah entered the foyer with Marshal Hastings close behind her. The interior was bedecked in burgundy, emerald green, and deep browns, filling every square inch of the Victorian house. In the parlor to Rebekah's right, an older man poured coffee. His badge introduced him as Marshal Wilde.

Rebekah's gaze swept the room. She caught sight of a woman perched on the end of a sofa amid delicately embroidered cushions. This was her patient.

Hands folded in her lap, the woman stared blankly at the wall. Honey blonde hair, hints of white feathering the natural curls around her face, was twisted in a severe bun at the nape of her neck. Her skin was pale as a porcelain doll, yet she held the look of a woman who had known hard work. And hard times.

Her blue eyes, though striking, were empty and watering. But Rebekah detected a spark of life beneath the dullness. Perhaps she could find a way to coax that life to the surface.

Rebekah went to the sofa and sat next to the woman, settling her medical bag on the floor. There was nothing in it to help this patient. She sensed that. Instead, she reached out and gently covered the woman's clenched hands with her own. They were cold to the touch. The woman didn't flinch, didn't indicate she felt anything.

Rebekah spoke softly. "Miss, I'm Doc Beck. Do you mind if I take a look at you?"

When she received no response, Rebekah shifted to look straight into the woman's face. With a thumb, she pulled down one eyelid, then the other. The woman blinked, but otherwise showed no reaction.

Rebekah turned back to the others in the room. Marshal Wilde and Marshal Hastings were standing close to the far wall, talking quietly. Wilde sipped coffee and avoided looking at the women. Hastings hadn't taken his eyes off them. Rebekah could feel it.

"Is she taking any medications?" she asked.

"Oh yes." Mrs. Wilde retrieved a pill bottle from the coffee stand and handed it to Rebekah. "Doctor Gleeson said she must take one of those every six hours. We didn't give her one in the middle of the first night and she woke up hysterical. We make sure she takes them properly now."

Rebekah accepted the bottle, turning it and noting the label. It was a mild sedative, not one that would put the woman in a frozen state like this. Which led her back to Doctor Gleeson's prognosis: The woman was incapable of caring for herself and needed to be placed in an asylum.

Sometimes Rebekah hated facts. Once the unidentified

woman was in, there was no getting out. But what if she had family?

Yet Rebekah knew that answer. When she boarded the stage-coach, the driver had asked her where she was traveling and why. He then told her he'd heard of the loco woman in Defiant Plains, and how Marshal Wilde sent telegrams to surrounding towns. They even posted notifications in local newspapers. No one claimed her after two days, and the woman had to be put some-where long-term besides the marshal's home.

Rebekah set the bottle aside and encased the woman's hands in her own, speaking directly to her. "You don't need to be afraid. I won't leave your side until you're taken care of."

There was no fear in the woman's eyes, no emotion at all. Rebekah squeezed the woman's hands, wishing she at least knew her name.

Rebekah started to rise but hesitated at the sound of soft tapping on the front door.

Mrs. Wilde went to answer it and let out a little gasp, backing away. A man came through the foyer, brushing past Mrs. Wilde to stand in the doorway of the parlor.

He by no means filled it, since he was barely taller than Rebekah, but his presence filled the room. Perhaps it was the fringed buckskin jacket he wore or his captivating gaze. But if Rebekah was a gambler, she would put her money on the two ivory handled six-guns snugged in black leather holsters that disturbed Mrs. Wilde.

Everything about the stranger marked him as a gunman, though perhaps past his prime. But Rebekah doubted anyone dared cross him. A sense of death came into the room with him. His soft expression and blue eyes were unnerving.

He looked directly at Rebekah, then his gaze shifted to the woman beside her. His whole being seemed to melt in an instant.

"Ella," he whispered, and the single word disrupted the room.

Mrs. Wilde gasped, "You know this woman?"

The man in the buckskin jacket didn't answer, just unstrapped his gun belt and dropped it to the floor. He took swift steps into the parlor, sweeping his hat off and going to one knee in front of the woman.

Rebekah still held the woman's hands protectively, and the nearness of this man jolted her. But she didn't pull away when he moved one hand to touch the woman's fingers beneath Rebekah's.

"She's...I'm her brother." His eyes searched the woman's motionless face, then looked to Rebekah, confusion clouding his sky-blue eyes. His voice was refined, even gentle. Not like most western men she encountered.

Rebekah said, "Her family was unknown. I'm a doctor, and I came to escort her to an asylum, but now that you're here, we can..."

Marshal Hastings, still standing near the wall, exploded in a burst of movement. He drew his six-gun, cocked it, and aimed it at the man kneeling in front of Rebekah.

Hastings shouted, "I recognize you! You're Cord Johnson, gun slick wanted for murder. You're under arrest."

Rebekah held in a gasp. *Cord Johnson.* Notorious gunman known from Arizona to South Dakota. In his heyday, it was said he wore two guns because there wasn't enough room for all his notches on one. Each notch represented a man killed.

Because of his nearness to the sofa, Rebekah could feel the muscles in Cord Johnson's body coiling. She suspected if he hadn't tossed aside his guns, he could kill Marshal Hastings, even though the man had the drop on him.

Instead, Cord Johnson glanced at the man over his shoulder, expression unchanging. But Rebekah imagined a hundred calculations going through the experienced gunman's mind.

He turned back to the woman, touching her fingers again. "Ella. It's me, Cord. Please tell them who I am so I can take you home."

A wash of relief flowed through Rebekah at the thought that

the woman had a home. But just as quickly, it was gone as she gazed down the barrel of Marshal Hastings' gun. He could well be pointing it at her with Cord Johnson positioned between her and the marshal, whose eyes were burning red.

"We know who you are," Hastings barked. "Now back away from those women, nice and slow."

Cord Johnson continued studying the woman's face, the one he called Ella, as if memorizing every line in it, to hold in his heart.

He could well be a murderer like Marshal Hastings said, but if he was, this woman, who he claimed was his sister, was his weak point.

Rebekah remained still, tense. The kneeling man could snatch her and use her as a shield while he drew the small pistol she detected tucked just out of sight in his waistline.

But he didn't.

Cord Johnson rose and faced the two marshals for the first time since entering the room. Rebekah didn't miss the light of recognition that flashed in Cord Johnson's eyes. He and Hastings knew each other, or at least, knew *of* each other.

Marshal Wilde also had his pistol out and motioned with it toward the door. "Let's go, Johnson. I'm sure I've got your wanted poster on my wall."

Cord Johnson allowed the marshal to lead him to the parlor door, and Rebekah noted his fleeting glance at his pistols on the floor. She imagined him making a dive for them, coming up and killing everyone in the room.

He didn't, but he did turn back to look Rebekah in the eyes.

"You are not taking my sister to an asylum."

CHAPTER 2

The return stagecoach ride was no easier on Rebekah than the one that carried her to Defiant Plains. If anything, it was harder because she carried a new burden—the responsibility of the woman called Ella and the strange appearance of a gunman who claimed to be her brother.

The name of Cord Johnson was known and feared throughout the west. At least, it had been several years ago. Gradually, people stopped hearing about him, stopped talking about him. Some guessed he was dead, others that he left the country, left his personal demons behind.

After the revelation in the Wildes' parlor that afternoon, Rebekah had wanted to hold off escorting her patient to the asylum. But Marshal Hastings argued that even if Cord Johnson was her brother, he was facing a noose. And the Wildes refused to keep Ella another night. Rebekah couldn't keep her at a hotel, pending who-knew-what.

It galled her to admit it, but Hastings was right. Cord Johnson's appearance changed nothing about her assignment to escort this woman to the Colorado State Insane Asylum.

Ella sat beside Rebekah now, hands limp in her lap, staring

blankly at the stagecoach wall. The two women were the only passengers.

Since they boarded the stage, Rebekah talked in a steady stream, observing the woman she decided to continue calling Ella. But there had been no response and it was time for the sedative.

In the rocking stage, Rebekah offered Ella the pill and water from the small canteen she kept in her medical bag. Ella didn't move and Rebekah prodded her before she finally placed the pill in her mouth and swallowed it with the water.

The woman obeyed like a trained dog, just as she had when they left the house and Rebekah coaxed her to board the stage. Her movements were mechanical, as though her brain were telling her what to do but her mind was gone.

Psychology wasn't Rebekah's field, though it was an interest. She wished she had taken more of an interest in it before now.

Within minutes, Ella was slumped low in the seat, her head resting in the corner, eyes closed. Rebekah retrieved her medical bag from under the seat and opened it. She found her small New Testament and began to read aloud.

"In the beginning was the Word, and the Word was with God, and the Word was God..."

Sometime later, Rebekah was on the third chapter of John and approaching her favorite childhood verse when a gunshot ripped the air. It echoed above the shouts of the driver and the thunder of the horses' hooves.

She hurriedly pocketed her Bible just as she felt the sharp pull-up of the horses. The stagecoach lurched forward, hard.

The sudden stop threw her across to the other seat, then the lurch back dumped her into the floorboard.

Ella had a similar experience, tangling with Rebekah and their skirts. Except Ella made no effort to straighten herself as she remained slouched against Rebekah.

There was eerie silence, then Rebekah heard the driver say, "I ain't carrying nothing valuable on this stage, mister."

A hold up.

Rebekah's medical bag had spilled out and Ella was partly seated on it. Rebekah pushed on the woman's shoulders to straighten her enough to pry the bag free.

She undid the latch on the false bottom of her bag, gripped her pepperbox pistol and aimed it over Ella's head at the stage-coach door just as the door was flung open.

Cord Johnson stood there, ivory handled six-guns out and cocked.

CHAPTER 3

Rebekah froze, pistol aimed but not cocked. Cord Johnson had one of his pistols pointing inside the stagecoach. Cocked.

He quickly took in the interior of the stage and, seeing only the two women, lifted the gun to point at the roof.

He uncocked and holstered it, his other pistol still aimed at the stagecoach driver. Cord Johnson extended his free hand toward Rebekah, not looking at her while he watched the driver.

"I'd take it kindly if you handed that pepperbox to me, ma'am."

Rebekah hesitated and Cord Johnson leaned into the stagecoach, gaze still trained on the driver. He wrapped his hand around the four barrels of the small pistol and tugged. Rebekah reluctantly released her grip. She wasn't prepared to shoot this man, or even threaten him.

He tucked the pepperbox in his gun belt then held his hand out again.

"Come, Ella. I'm taking you home."

The woman didn't move. Cord Johnson, smooth and easy, reached into the coach and wrapped his arm under Ella's arms and

18

pulled her forward. He swung her out of the coach but Ella's foot caught on the doorway, sending her flying.

Rebekah scrambled out, darting down the steps underneath Cord Johnson's gun. He had broken Ella's fall and lowered her to the ground. Rebekah knelt beside her patient where she lay limp in the dust.

A shot sounded, causing Rebekah's ears to ring as the bullet struck the dirt near her. Cord Johnson returned fire at the stage-coach driver and the team of horses took off at a run. Cord Johnson fired two more shots in the air and the stage didn't stop.

Rebekah lifted Ella by the shoulders, turning her face up. The woman's legs sprawled in front of her, skirts fluttering above her knees in the wind.

Cord Johnson holstered his pistol and knelt on Ella's other side. He tugged her skirts down and tucked the cotton material underneath her ankles. Then he looked at Rebekah.

"I didn't mean for you to get in the middle of this, Doctor."

Rebekah met Cord Johnson's gaze. Foolish or not, she didn't fear him. "I go where I'm needed."

Whatever you do, stay out of trouble. Her uncle Robert's words taunted Rebekah now as she glanced around the deserted road guarded only by the distant Rocky Mountains. In the other direction, the stagecoach had disappeared over the horizon. The driver wasn't coming back for her.

That meant she wouldn't have her medical bag and Ella's medicine when she needed it. She recalled what Mrs. Wilde said about Ella's hysterics. Time was ticking down from the six-hour mark.

She cradled Ella around the shoulders and gave the woman a squeeze. "Something tells me this woman needs me very much."

Cord Johnson turned to Ella and took one of her hands in his as he spoke to Rebekah. "Stay here on the road, Doctor. There will be a wagon along sometime soon or another stage."

Even as he said it, Rebekah detected the doubt in his voice.

Rebekah brushed Ella's honey-blonde hair back from her face and tucked it behind her ears. The woman's bun had loosened in the jarring and she lost her hat. Rebekah had lost hers as well, and she was aware of her long brown hair being blown loose.

"Be that as it may, I must stay with my patient."

Cord Johnson rose and gently took Ella under the arms again, helping her up. Rebekah stood as well, keeping a supporting hand on the woman's back. The sedative made her unsteady.

Cord Johnson nodded toward the ravine by the road. "I suppose the wagon is big enough to carry the three of us to Stark's Crossing. You can take a train home from there, wherever home is for you."

Such a simple statement, but it struck Rebekah hard.

There wasn't time to worry about the trouble she was getting into. Glancing over her shoulder, she spotted a wagon and team waiting in the gully. From there, the semblance of a trail led away from the main road and, difficult as it was to believe, would be an even rougher ride.

When Rebekah turned back, Cord had her pepperbox in hand. He held it by the barrel, offering Rebekah the butt end.

"You may need this," he said quietly. "A woman should have a way to defend herself."

Rebekah wrapped her fingers around the familiar handle, wondering why she felt inclined to trust this man.

Perhaps it was true, what newspapermen used to say, that Cord Johnson's voice was mesmerizing. Vocal honey, one reporter wrote, then added, *but if it catches you, you're like a fly in a spider's web, and just as good as dead.*

THE CANYON they traveled through was desert-like, bringing back unpleasant memories for Rebekah. But she restrained those to focus on someone undergoing a greater trial—Ella.

When they halted for a rest, she barely ate of the modest fare Cord Johnson had packed. As they continued on, Rebekah sensed restlessness in the woman. It had been over six hours since her last pill.

Rebekah rode in the bed with Ella, watching the passing terrain and observing the vegetation on the low rim of the canyon. She grabbed the back of the wagon seat and pulled herself up, body swaying with the wagon while she spoke to Cord Johnson.

"I need you to stop. I have to find something."

Cord glanced back. "You lost something?"

Rebekah braced against the wagon seat. "Just stop, please."

He pulled back on the reins with a *whoa*. The stillness was a blessed relief after bouncing in the back of the wagon for hours over terrain never intended to be a road.

Cord shifted on the seat, one hand resting on the back as he observed Ella. He still wore his six guns and Rebekah noticed how he always scanned the horizon all around them. He was a man who lived life looking over his shoulder, especially with abducting two women.

Except Rebekah could hardly call herself a captive since she was armed with her pepperbox. She'd checked to ensure it still had bullets in it. Cord Johnson had returned her loaded gun and trusted her not to use it on him. Was it because he wanted to trick her into trusting him?

Rebekah wasn't sure how she felt about this quiet man—a deadly killer. His unmistakable buckskin jacket had once struck fear in the hearts of anyone who encountered him—no matter which side of the law they were on. He played the role of a hired gunman, and one who killed whenever he was challenged.

But he expressed none of this as he glanced down at Ella, who shivered beneath a blanket despite the warmth of day still around her.

"What can you do for her, Doctor?"

Rebekah gathered her skirts and prepared to climb out of the wagon. "Chamomile tea will help calm her nerves."

Cord Johnson set the wagon brake and tied the reins around it before jumping off the wagon with cat-like swiftness. He offered to help Rebekah down. She let him, bracing her hands on his shoulders as he swung her from the wagon to the ground.

He was stronger than he looked, standing eye to eye with Rebekah as she caught her balance. He had the stature of someone not afraid of a hard day's work on a farm. That didn't exactly fit his profile as a gunfighter, or a man wanted for murder.

In the back of the wagon, Ella moaned. She was waking.

Cord Johnson released Rebekah and she took a step back, then hurried to scramble up to the rim of the canyon. She needed to focus on finding chamomile flowers and tending to Ella.

Time was up.

CHAPTER 4

By the time Rebekah returned to the wagon, the sun had slipped below the Rockies, and the high peaks had no trouble bedding the sun down.

A bouquet of daisy-like flowers in hand, Rebekah found her way by the tiny flames of the fire Cord Johnson tended where he set up camp next to the wagon. He had positioned a coffee pot on rocks near the flames, his gun belt placed neatly on his empty bedroll.

Ella laid curled on another bedroll near the fire, tears streaking her face but otherwise, she was silent. Perhaps the trip would help her regain her senses, if that were still possible. Rebekah needed Ella to identify or deny that Cord Johnson was her brother.

He stood as Rebekah entered the camp, though she doubted he was surprised. In fact, she doubted he'd lost track of her for a moment, his keen senses as much a part of him as his neutral expression. The only time she saw real change in it was when he looked at Ella.

Rebekah nodded at the pot. "I'll need hot water, not coffee."

"It's plain water in the pot. Should be boiling in a few minutes."

Rebekah knelt beside Ella, laying the flowers on the blanket beside her. She brushed aside loose hair from Ella's forehead and touched it with the back of her hand. The woman was hot to the touch even as the day cooled into evening.

Rebekah frowned. "She shouldn't have this kind of reaction from not taking the sedative."

Cord squatted beside her. "Will your tea help?"

"It should."

If only Rebekah knew what had taken place that put Ella in her current state.

Rebekah began plucking white petals from the yellow center of one flower. "Do you know what happened to her exactly?"

She heard Cord Johnson's deep sigh behind her, as though he were taking in and releasing a lifetime of regrets.

"It's a long story, Doctor."

Rebekah shifted so that she could continue plucking petals as she watched him, close behind her where he was seated beside Ella, not taking his eyes off her sweating face.

"I do believe we have the time, Mr. Johnson."

The gunman leaned forward to stroke Ella's hair. Her eyes slowly closed.

Cord said quietly, "It's hard to take, her not knowing me."

Rebekah gathered the petals in her hands, holding them loosely while she waited for the water to boil.

"There is a great deal we do not yet know about the human brain, and how the mind works. If she suffered trauma, that could explain her behavior. Or has she been this way for some time?"

He shook his head. "Two months ago, you would have never met a stronger woman with a good head on her shoulders. But... I'm not surprised she's refusing to acknowledge me. I failed her."

The water in the pot sounded close to boiling, but Rebekah

didn't move, didn't want to disturb the release of what she felt was a difficult story.

He spoke slow and purposeful, as if choosing each word after long consideration. "She took care of the family farm for years. Finished raising me after our parents died. She brooked no nonsense, but she showed me what love truly was. After my years of...I'm sure you heard enough from Marshal Hastings. But even after that, she took me back in. She always looked after her baby brother. Even when I didn't deserve it."

When the silence lengthened, Rebekah said, "No one deserves grace, Mr. Johnson. Otherwise, it wouldn't be grace."

The gunman met her gaze and Rebekah caught her breath. No wonder men lost their lives under this steady look. But Cord Johnson wasn't going to take her life. She saw that, too, and heard it in his next words.

"Do you believe in complete redemption, Doctor?"

His question caught her off guard. She did believe in redemption, but for now, it was more important to determine if she could believe and trust this man.

"Do you believe in it, Mr. Johnson?"

"I did. For a time. Ella convinced me. Yet I wonder if a man will always revert to what he truly is."

He rested his fingertips on Ella's trembling hand. "We had a quiet life, quiet evenings where we'd sit after a long day's work and just be together. Like we were making up for those years we missed, and there was no hurry to do it."

Rebekah nearly lost her breath again, this time from the fire of pain in her heart. He could have been describing her young life, evenings in the log cabin that she relished with her father, sipping tea and reflecting on the day.

Those days long, long ago. When he passed, she spent those evenings alone. Then tragedy took her away from the home hearth completely.

This wasn't the time to dwell on those memories. The water

was boiling and she had a patient to tend. Rebekah used her handkerchief to lift the lid on the coffee pot and dropped the white petals in.

"And those quiet evenings with Ella were taken away?"

She didn't want to think on how getting involved with Cord Johnson and Ella was threatening her attempt to return to that fireside of her life.

Cord Johnson drew his knees up and rested his forearms on them, clenching his hands into fists. "We traveled into Cimarron like we did every second Thursday of the month. I went to the hardware store for fencing supplies while she took our calf cash money to the bank." He paused, then spoke in a deeper tone, as though living the day all over again.

"I heard shooting and screams, but by the time I ran out of the warehouse, the outlaws were already mounted. Though he was masked, I knew the leader was Buck Callaghan by the gang's reputation. He had Ella across his saddle. He wanted to use her to catch bullets if anyone tried to stop them."

Rebekah swallowed, recalling the moment Cord Johnson entered Marshal Wilde's house. The moment he saw Ella seated next to Rebekah.

"I hadn't strapped on my double pistols in fifteen years, but I carried a pistol in my belt, and Ella never minded that. She knew I would only use it to protect her."

He closed his eyes. "I fired at the man on the right. I hoped he would turn his horse in the pathway of Buck Callaghan, and it worked. But the sheriff and townspeople started shooting, and Callaghan spun away to fire back. He shot me in the arm and leg, and the last thing I remember was seeing my sister's face, pleading for me to save her. I didn't."

Cord Johnson opened his eyes, bringing time forward. "After a week, the posse gave up, figuring Ella was already dead and the money gone forever. But I strapped on my pistols as soon as I could walk. I swore I wouldn't take them off until I found her."

The thump of the double pistols hitting the floor of the Wilde's parlor rang in Rebekah's memory. If this gunman wasn't telling the truth, he knew how to make the pieces of a lie fit together perfectly.

Cord Johnson went on. "It took a month of tracking down those outlaws one by one before I finally discovered she was near Defiant Plains."

His eyes cleared and he stared straight at Rebekah. "I started out life as a farmer. I ended up a gunman. But I've never killed anyone in cold blood."

Rebekah knew he was waiting for her acknowledgment, to show she either believed he was guilty of murder or not.

She wasn't ready to decide that, but as she poured the tea into a tin cup, she said, "It's been a great deal of time since I've seen my own brother."

Rebekah moved back to Ella, who was shivering. Rebekah directed Cord to prop her up enough to receive a few sips of tea. Ella, eyes squeezed shut, started to refuse more, but Rebekah was able to coax her to drink the whole mug.

Ella swallowed a final time, and Cord Johnson carefully laid her head onto the makeshift pillow. He undid his bandana and dabbed her sweaty forehead. When Rebekah looked up, her gaze caught on a glint of gold at his neck, previously covered by the bandana.

He was aware of her noticing even though Rebekah looked away quickly. Did this man not miss even an eyelash quiver?

Cord Johnson laid the bandanna aside and used both hands to draw the long chain up, a pendant coming out from under his shirt. It was a gold locket.

He opened the locket with his fingernail and held it toward the light for Rebekah to see. "This belongs to Ella. It was a miracle someone found it in the bank after the robbery and gave it to me."

Rebekah leaned forward, squinting at the two black-and-white images inside the locket. One was of a handsome young couple dressed in simple prairie-style clothing, posed with children. A little boy in a long white nightgown and bonnet sat in the woman's lap while a girl in a knee-length dress stood with her hand resting on the woman's shoulder. The man, though young, looked hard and stern.

Opposite that family portrait was one that made Rebekah scoot closer to inspect. It was a teenage boy in his Sunday best, Derby hat tucked under his arm and facing straight at the camera, eyes and expression neutral but tender. Innocent. Familiar.

Rebekah glanced up to compare the image with Cord Johnson's face and realized she was close. Too close.

She quickly leaned back, blinked, then looked between the image and him. It was a match. And she could no longer deny the similarities of his thin, wispy blonde hair and her patient's.

Cord Johnson was telling the truth: Ella was his sister.

That didn't answer the question of whether or not he was wanted for murder, but it did tell Rebekah she needed to get this woman well. And home.

Whatever you do, stay out of trouble.

It might not be possible to follow her uncle's advice this time. She was, after all, of the upstream people. She would not be afraid to move against the flow to do the work she felt God calling her to do.

CHAPTER 5

Mercifully, the tea mixture gave Ella a night's rest and in turn, Rebekah one as well. They needed it for the next day that stretched into a long one with Rebekah riding in the back of the wagon once again with Ella, Cord Johnson driving the team over rough country.

The gunman was still awake when Rebekah drifted off last night, and he was awake the next morning, a pot of hot water ready to brew Ella more tea. Rebekah wondered how many sleepless nights he endured in the hunt for his sister.

One thing she'd decided in the night: She believed Cord Johnson when he said he had never killed anyone in cold blood.

But as long as Rebekah was with Cord and Ella Johnson, she was on the wrong side of the law. What if news of Cord Johnson escaping jail with his sister and a woman doctor exploded across the state? Few things could be worse for Rebekah before her meeting with Senator Harris and the governor of Nebraska.

But she couldn't abandon this brother and sister.

As the sun climbed the sky, Rebekah draped a blanket across the bed of the wagon to give her and Ella shade on their hatless heads. She spent the hours reading to Ella and observing change in her. The tea sedative was equivalent to the pill she had been taking, but Ella's demeanor was slowly changing. Her face was no longer frozen in a blank stare. It softened and gave her the same kind of expression as her brother. But she still didn't speak nor acknowledge Rebekah's presence.

They halted for the noon meal and a rest. Rebekah contemplated not giving her patient the tea, and let her come to a fully conscious state. But Rebekah's instincts told her the woman wasn't ready for that. They needed to get out of this wilderness and settled in a good place for both Ella and Cord Johnson to sort out their lives. And the only place Rebekah could see for that was their home.

After the meal, the trio set out again. The tea made Ella sleep and gave Rebekah a chance to rest as well. Hers became a deep sleep, and sometime later, Rebekah awoke disoriented. It took her a few moments to realize they were coming to a halt.

Rebekah propped up on her elbow as she rubbed her eyes. The jingle of chains sounded as Cord Johnson undid the tailgate latches and lowered it. He crawled into the wagon and back to where the women were.

He nodded at Ella. "How is she, Doctor?"

Rebekah observed her patient. Ella was sleeping soundly, and seemed at peace.

"We should let her sleep as long as possible."

Cord Johnson didn't take his eyes off his sister as he adjusted loose hair off her neck where it raised sweat. "Thank you for caring for her, Doctor...I'm afraid I don't even know your name."

"I suppose we never were properly introduced, though you needed no introduction."

His expression didn't change, but Rebekah regretted her offhand comment as soon as she said it. She hurried on. "I'm Doctor Rebekah LaRoche. But that is quite a mouthful, so many in the west call me Doc Beck."

She shifted to try and see the countryside they had covered. "Where are we?"

"Stark's Crossing."

Rebekah sat up in a hurry, catching her head in the blanket and bringing it down around her. She struggled to get out from underneath it until Cord Johnson freed her. She combed fingers through her dirty hair, knowing it was quite a mess.

"We've made it to Stark's Crossing?" That had to be over forty miles from where they started.

Cord Johnson was a determined man.

He shifted, nodding over her shoulder. "We can take the train straight to Cimarron from here."

Beyond the copse of trees where the wagon was sheltered lay a town of middling size. Large enough for a railroad station, along with shops where Rebekah could get a fresh change of clothes.

Though she'd unintentionally left her carpetbag and medical bag on the stage, she had money sewed inside the pocket of her skirt. Clean clothes would be lovely before a train ride.

"You said your farm is near Cimarron? In Kansas?"

"Yes, ma'am."

"You're a long way from home, Mr. Johnson."

"There were times I was even further away."

A whistle sounded, announcing a train arriving at the depot. They didn't have time to catch it and Rebekah doubted they should. She turned back to Cord Johnson, still combing fingers through her thick hair.

"If Marshal Wilde sent a wire to other authorities, someone could be on the look-out for three dusty-faced vagrants in Stark's Crossing. Why don't I go into town and pick out suitable clothing —disguises if you will—for the trip? We look like outlaws on the run."

Cord straightened enough to pull a wallet from his trouser pocket. "Could you find Ella something as well?"

He handed Rebekah several bills which she tucked deep in her pocket.

"Of course. Why don't you get a hotel room..." She quickly added, "...two hotel rooms and I will meet you both there. I'll purchase the train tickets, too. The less you and Ella are seen, the better."

CHAPTER 6

Thankfully, the town was large enough for a seamstress shop with ready-made clothing. They certainly wouldn't look tailor-made, but Rebekah selected fine outfits for herself and the Johnsons. If they wanted to appear inconspicuous, the best way was to look like well-prepared travelers.

She needed to give Ella a healthy dose of the tea before they boarded the train. A woman in hysterics would draw the kind of attention they needed to avoid.

Rebekah had enough money to cover the clothing, shoes, and hats with just enough left over to buy train tickets. She hoped Cord Johnson had more bills in his wallet. This was turning out to be a more expensive trip than Rebekah planned for.

In more ways than one.

Since it was impossible for Rebekah to carry all of the packages by herself to the hotel, she agreed with the seamstress's offer to have them delivered within the hour.

Rebekah opted to take two of the packages, new undergarments, with her while she went to the train depot to purchase tickets for the next train east to Cimarron, Kansas. But she hesitated there about another item of business.

By now, Marshal Wilde or the stage driver might have wired McKinnon Ranch with the news that Rebekah was abducted by a highwayman.

Though she was committed to helping Cord and Ella Johnson get home, Rebekah decided to risk a telegram. In the past few months alone, she'd put enough strain on her uncle Robert to last a lifetime.

She settled on a simple message: *I am well. Please do not worry for me. Becka.*

The telegram took the last of Rebekah's cash, but it was worth it to set his mind at ease. Unless he misunderstood and notified Marshal Wilde of her location. That was a worry since the train east wouldn't leave until eight the next morning.

But there was no point in fretting over it. Rebekah exited the depot and drew in a deep breath. Evening was coming and the sunset bathing Stark's Crossing was gorgeous, a striking peach and pink that filled the entire western sky. Rebekah wanted to stand there until the last trace disappeared and twilight came.

But the thought of a hot bath and sleeping in a real bed lured her down the sidewalk toward the hotel two blocks from the depot. And Rebekah needed to brew Ella another cup of tea.

The boardwalk lowered down three steps for a short stretch to the next building. This part of the walk looked as if it washed out often, leaving the wood boards uneven. Rebekah carefully picked her way over it, holding the boxes to one side so she could see where to place her feet.

She had almost crossed the open space between the buildings when someone stepped from the shadows and grabbed her wrist.

Rebekah yelped as a man swung her into the alleyway and pushed her against the mercantile wall. She looked up, ready to scream, but froze in shock. It was Marshal Hastings.

CHAPTER 7

Few things could have shocked Rebekah more than seeing this U.S. Marshal in front of her, his cool grey eyes staring her down. How could he have gotten to Stark's Crossing so fast from Defiant Plains? Most of all, *why* was he there?

Hastings put one hand on the wall by Rebekah's head. "Fancy seeing you here, Doc Beck. Been doing a little shopping?"

He nodded to the packages he'd knocked to the ground while accosting her.

Rebekah swallowed. She hadn't trusted this man from the moment she met him and she didn't trust him now. Was he hunting Cord Johnson? Did he suspect Rebekah knew where the gunman was?

Hastings must have disembarked from the train earlier, and somehow missed Cord and Ella sneaking into the hotel.

Though for all Rebekah knew, they were still in the woods with the wagon. Cord Johnson had hesitated about her hotel idea, reluctant to enter Stark's Crossing in the daylight.

Well, it was nearing dark now and Rebekah could use some

help. But there was none at hand, so she straightened her shoulders and took a side-step away from Marshal Hastings.

"If you'll excuse me..."

Marshal Hastings' free hand shot out, flattening against the wall on the other side of her head. She was trapped.

His chilling smile was gone, replaced by a deadly look. "Where are they?"

On the boardwalk, two ladies passed by. One glanced their way and Rebekah contemplated screaming for help. But the woman covered her mouth and whispered something to her companion. The two hurried on.

What could Rebekah do? If she called out, Hastings would flash his U.S. Marshal badge and land Rebekah right where she didn't want—in the middle of a public scene.

Besides, she had a few questions of her own.

Trying not to show how she trembled, Rebekah looked Hastings in the eyes as he towered over her.

"You're a long way from the last place I saw you, Marshal. What brought you to Stark's Crossing?"

Hastings leaned closer and Rebekah turned her face away, breathing shallow. He whispered close to her ear, "I'm in charge, little lady doctor. And you're under arrest."

No! Rebekah screamed inside. This couldn't be. She'd never been arrested in her life.

It was time to take desperate measures.

Rebekah twisted, drawing her elbow up and shoving it into Marshal Hastings' gut. He gasped and doubled over.

She hadn't taken two steps, though, when Hastings snagged her arm and halted her flight.

He snarled, "I would add assaulting a federal officer to your list of charges, but I'll stick with kidnapping a crazy woman and helping a wanted murderer escape."

His fingernails dug into her arm through her navy jacket and Rebekah gritted her teeth.

"There is nothing illegal about reuniting a brother and sister."

The face of her own brother flashed through her mind and she whispered, "At least, there shouldn't be."

But Marshal Hastings wasn't interested in hearing her side of things. Rebekah's mind swirled with what he had said. Kidnapping Ella? Would he really charge her with such a crime? And why did the marshal assume she was helping Cord Johnson get away? For all he knew, Rebekah had escaped the highway man on her own and made it to Stark's Crossing...

But that notion was absurd even to her. She wouldn't have traveled all this way on her own across rugged terrain. And to be right on the pathway of Cord and Ella's home...

That left the question of how Marshal Hastings knew they'd be there. If he believed Cord Johnson was a murderer, why would he suspect the gunman was heading to Cimarron after breaking jail?

These questions occupied Rebekah as Hastings dragged her across town to a building marked JAIL.

The cold word encased her heart in a block of ice. Surely she wasn't really and truly being arrested?

Inside, a deputy had his feet propped on the desk, snoring. Hastings slammed the door closed behind Rebekah, making both her and the deputy jump.

He stood quickly, off balance as he blinked rapidly as though resisting rubbing the sleep out of his eyes. He brushed his hair back and settled his hat on his head.

"Marshal Hastings. What have you got here?"

So, the marshal had already been there, probably alerting the local law-enforcement of the trio of lawbreakers—a female doctor, a woman heading for an asylum, and a reformed gunman.

Rebekah hoped Cord Johnson hadn't followed her advice and gotten hotel rooms already. How could she warn him to stay out of town? But then, did she need to?

Cord Johnson was extraordinarily observant and watched

every shadow while thinking about shadows that might still lie ahead. It was the only way he could have survived his days as a gunman.

Marshal Hastings answered the deputy, "Got a prisoner for you, Bob. This is the woman that kidnapped the poor crazy woman and helped Cord Johnson escape. I need you to lock her up while I search for Johnson."

The deputy's eyes grew round. He was young and skinny and she doubted he'd had his first barbershop shave. "But...but..." He looked at Rebekah. "Ain't you Doc Beck, the famous woman doctor that saved them girls down in New Mexico?"

So, Michael Hamilton's article about Rebekah had reached Stark's Crossing. She wasn't surprised since the AP reporter sent the news out to every newspaper that had a connection to the outside world. For once, Rebekah was grateful for Michael Hamilton's inflated article about the incident at the mission.

Before Hastings could answer, Rebekah rushed to say, "I am, and this marshal has no right to arrest me. I would take it kindly if you told this man to take his hands off me."

Deputy Bob's eyes grew even rounder and Rebekah feared they would pop out of their sockets.

Hastings glanced down at her with his chilling smile, understanding exactly what she was doing. "Bob, when you pinned on that badge, you took an oath to uphold the law. The law says you got to lock this woman up."

Hastings shoved Rebekah toward the side door that opened to iron cells. "Now do your duty."

Deputy Bob stepped around the desk, his fingers brushing the huge key ring that lay on it. He looked hesitantly between Rebekah and Marshal Hastings.

"But I ain't never... It don't seem right, locking up a woman. Them cells... all kinds of men have been in there..."

Hastings shouted, "Do your duty!"

Deputy Bob recoiled, taking a step back and tripping on the

edge of the desk. He caught himself and scrambled to grab the keys. He didn't meet Rebekah's pleading gaze as he went into the back and swung open the door to one of two empty cells.

Hastings followed, Rebekah in tow. He shoved her and Rebekah stumbled. Deputy Bob reached out to catch her, then guided her into the cell. He closed the door, the clink loud and final.

He looked through the bars, his eyes pools of sadness. "I'm sorry about this, Doc Beck. I'm just doing my duty."

This deputy might as well be a parrot. Maybe she could get him to say or do something useful. Rebekah grabbed the bars.

"Please wire Doctor McKinnon at McKinnon Ranch in Centennial Ridge and tell him where I am."

But as soon as the words came out of her mouth, Rebekah wished them back. She shook her head. "No, never mind. Don't wire anyone. I don't want anyone to know I am...that I've been arrested. But please, you cannot keep me here. I want to see the sheriff..."

Marshal Hastings snatched the back of Deputy Bob's collar and dragged him from the room. He slammed the door, cutting Rebekah off from any chance of sweet-talking the deputy.

With a heavy sigh, Rebekah leaned her forehead on the cold bars of the cell door.

Whatever you do, stay out of trouble.

CHAPTER 8

Since this was the first time for Rebekah inside a jail cell as a prisoner, she wasn't quite sure what to do. She called for the deputy, but he either couldn't hear her or was too embarrassed to come.

As a prisoner, she expected to at least be fed and preferably given something to read. But when Deputy Bob didn't heed her repeated calls, she settled on the edge of the cot. From the look of the blanket, this wasn't a place to get the rest she needed. She'd rather curl up in the corner of the cell than sleep on the cot.

At least she had her small New Testament in her pocket. She'd read it more in the past two days than the past several years. It was like becoming reacquainted with a lost, beloved friend.

But at the moment, it was hard to concentrate on reading. Thoughts of Cord Johnson and his sister occupied her mind. She wondered how Ella was doing, and if Cord had given her another serving of the tea. Rebekah had left fresh petals in a pouch in the wagon, but it could have gotten left behind if they were already at the hotel.

What would happen once Ella was free from being in a stupor?

That brought Rebekah back to the question of the pills. The mild sedative should have had virtually the same effect on Ella as the tea, but the pills seemed to make her brain only function enough to perform essentials. Unless it was true, and Ella really had lost her mind.

Rebekah studied the solid stone and barred walls holding her, tracing the cracks in the mortar from the hastily constructed jail like many buildings in the west. But it was solid and made her wonder how Cord Johnson managed to escape jail back in Defiant Plains.

This place seemed impenetrable. Her only hope was talking that young deputy into releasing her before she had to go before a judge and explained why she was helping an accused murderer abduct his sister.

That would be a very public scene.

Rebekah's thoughts turned again to Ella, or that was where she thought they were going.

But her mind wandered down another path, an ancient yet a modern one, the one she had walked all of her life...until recent years.

It was the path of her people, the Omaha, the upstream people, who had lived and hunted on this land from time immemorial.

But change came to her people before Rebekah was born. Her father taught her about that change and she longed to follow in his footsteps on that ancient yet modern path. But somewhere, she lost her way.

It started that fateful winter night in her office near Macy on the Omaha Indian Reservation...

THE COLD WAS bitter as Rebekah closed the windows in the exam room. She'd just finished giving it a disinfecting scrub and she always opened the windows no matter how cold it was on the Nebraskan prairie. She often did the same when performing surgery to keep the chloroform from dulling her senses while she worked.

That day, she had to clean the patient room after amputating a young boy's leg. It was an emotionally difficult operation, to remove a vital limb from a boy just beginning his life. But the deep cut he'd suffered had gotten infected and turned to gangrene. By the time his family brought him to Rebekah, she was in time to save his life, but not his leg.

And that had been Rebekah's eighth patient of the long day.

The patients didn't always come to her. In fact, they rarely did. She found herself bundling into her buggy more often than not, traversing the frozen prairie to answer a loved one's call for a patient who needed her. Now, though, it was time to rest. She was tired.

But as Rebekah locked the last window against the retreating storm, looking forward to a good night's sleep, sounds of a wagon and team told her this wasn't the night for it.

Rebekah stepped into her main office as a door banged open and a man staggered in backwards. He was shuffling under the weight of carrying a man under the arms while another man, who Rebekah recognized was Charlie, had the unconscious man's legs. Together, they managed to weave inside her small office.

They lowered the big man to the floor near the potbelly stove and Rebekah gasped. It was Indian Agent Roger Graham.

While Charlie went outside again, the first man straightened and pushed his hat up his forehead despite how it was tied down with a scarf. His thin, long brown-black hair spread out from beneath his winter wrappings. But Rebekah had known from the moment the door opened that the man was her only sibling. Asa.

She spoke in Omaha. "What happened, brother?"

Asa nodded at the man on the floor. "Buggy accident. The creek." Even the few words drew out a hard cough from her brother. She didn't want to think about what that meant. She knew too well.

There was no time for further questions. Asa headed back out as Charlie, the middle-aged Omaha man she'd known all her life, returned, carrying a wrapped bundle. It was Mrs. Graham.

Rebekah pointed to the exam room. "Take her in there, please."

Before Rebekah could go to either the woman or the unconscious Indian agent, Asa came to the door and turned sideways to get through with his own blanket-wrapped bundle.

Rebekah saw it was Agent Graham's ten-year-old daughter, Bethany. Her blonde hair was matted with blood from a cut on her forehead.

Rebekah directed Asa to take her into the exam room as well while she returned to Agent Graham. She noted the large lump on the back of his head which had rendered him unconscious. She didn't detect any broken ribs which helped relieve the threat of internal bleeding.

After her precursor examination, she called for Charlie to stay with the agent and build up the fire in the stove while she hurried into the exam room.

The little girl, Bethany, was laid out on the table, moaning. Asa stood near where Mrs. Graham was propped in a chair by the wall. Rebekah went to the woman, intending to see if she should be laying down, too. But the woman flung her hand out to stop Rebekah, then pointed a long, slender finger at the girl.

"Not me! Save my daughter, please!"

The fact that the woman could sit up and talk was a good enough sign.

Rebekah turned from her and went to the little girl. She began unwrapping the blankets she'd been rolled in. Bethany was wet and shivering, but what concerned Rebekah was the blood soaking her blue gingham fabric over her stomach.

Something had punctured her deeply and with only one

glance, Rebekah knew the situation was dire. The cold had slowed the bleeding, but Bethany had lost a tremendous amount of blood. There was only one way to possibly save her.

"Charlie! Come in here."

Rebekah opened her medical bag where she kept her double-ended blood transfusion apparatus for emergencies only. This qualified.

But jingling from the team of horses answered her. Asa coughed and said quietly, "He goes to Bancroft for the doctor."

Rebekah brought her gaze up sharply to her brother, who was across the table, watching her. Mrs. Graham was doubled over, sobbing and moaning.

Instead of questioning Asa, she glanced over her shoulder at the unconscious Agent Graham on the office floor. Of course the agent would have insisted the Omaha Indian men take his family to be treated in Bancroft even though it was much further away. There wasn't time for that, and Asa knew it.

Rebekah dipped the hypodermic needles of the transfusion apparatus in a bottle of pharmaceutical alcohol. She spoke to Asa without meeting his eyes. "I will need your help, if you are willing. Roll up your sleeve."

Asa was willing, but twenty minutes later, Rebekah knew it hadn't worked. She felt the moment life went out of the child's body. Bethany's chest lowered in one final breath, and Rebekah, hands covered in blood, pressed against the little girl's still heart.

Rebekah let out her own grievous breath, eyes closed. She had known this child only a few months. Not long at all.

Asa coughed and Rebekah removed the needle from his arm where she'd tried to transfer his blood to save the little girl. Asa tugged the blanket over the little girl's face.

Mrs. Graham wailed and slumped to the floor.

Before Rebekah could go to her, a primal scream froze her body and heart.

"No!"

Agent Graham filled the doorway of the exam room, eyes like a wild beast. His three-piece suit was torn, the gray material stained with splotches of blood. He pressed both hands against the doorframe, staring at the blanket covered form.

"No."

His arms shook then he leveled Rebekah with those wild eyes. "You."

In that single word was packed all the distain Indian Agent Roger Graham held for Rebekah since he was placed over the reservation four months ago. He objected to women doctors, especially the first Indian ones, and insisted Rebekah never treat white patients. If her own people wanted her, fine. But he made his position clear. He didn't like her. And now, judging from the look in his eyes, he hated her.

His voice was raspy, uncontrolled. "Get away from my daughter! Get away!"

He lunged into the room and fell to his knees. He forced himself up and sprawled across the body of his little girl, weeping.

Rebekah swallowed, her practiced eye going to the lump at the back of his head. She needed to treat him, but she could do nothing for his broken heart. "I'm sorry, Agent Graham. She lost too much blood. I am so sorry."

Agent Graham reared back, swinging his arm wildly at Rebekah. She moved back out of reach as Asa took a step forward. Graham swept his arm again. "You Indians will pay dearly. You both will."

Soon, Charlie would return with the doctor from Bancroft. There was little more she could do except await Agent Graham's wrath.

❦

IN THE DEEP state of her memories, Rebekah realized she had resorted to curling atop the dirty blanket on the cot in the jail cell. She wiped moisture from her face, but she could not wipe away that fateful night, the one that set her on her current path.

Rebekah had lost patients before. But none quite so devastating for her and her people as when little Bethany passed, and a short time later, Mrs. Graham.

Rebekah's heart grieved for the deceased and for loved ones they left behind. And she grieved for how it cost her people one of their precious few resources for medical care.

After she was barred from the reservation with the threat that if she'd ever returned, she'd have her medical license revoked, Rebekah went to the only other family she could—her uncle Robert McKinnon.

As her stepmother's brother, Rebekah spent part of her summers at his ranch in Wyoming during her growing up years. Doctor McKinnon later became her primary sponsor for medical school, and she could never repay what she owed him in her life. But she knew she didn't need to. They were truly family.

As much as she and her brother Asa were family, no matter the miles and years and threats that kept them apart. Even after he had chosen to live among the traditional Omahas like Charlie, away from where he was raised in the 'village of the make-believe white men,' she and Asa spoke a language others couldn't understand. It was neither Omaha, nor English, nor French. It was one of family.

She could see herself now, standing at her family home, in the cabin doorway. Asa helping her load her bags in her buggy. While it was taking all of Rebekah's willpower to leave the Omaha Indian Reservation, it took all her heart, too.

Standing there, staring at one another, Asa finally said, "Our people need you."

Her brother—who'd never been in favor of adopting white ways, had not spoken English since he'd become a man, did not like Rebekah assimilating through education and friends—had in four simple words acknowledged everything she'd worked for.

But it was everything he didn't say that ripped Rebekah's heart out.

Your family needs you. We love you. Do not go.

In that moment, lying on the cot in the jail cell, Rebekah never felt further away from her brother and the echo of her people's cry.

"Doc Beck. We need you."

Rebekah heard an echo of the whisper and realized she was really hearing a voice. But it wasn't Deputy Bob.

Rebekah pushed up on the cot, legs still curled beneath her. She glanced around the empty room.

Then the voice whispered, "Be ready, Doctor."

Rebekah glanced up at the barred window far above her head to see a shadow disappearing. She wiped her eyes clear, then got to her feet, going to the window.

It was too high to see out of and she looked around for something to stand on. There was a wooden stool in the cell and she used it but still, the top of her head barely reached the barred window.

She gripped the bars and tried to pull herself up, but racket from behind distracted her. Muffled sounds came from the sheriff's office, then the door to the cells opened.

Cord Johnson appeared, huge key ring in hand.

Rebekah was so surprised, she released the window bars. The stool went out from beneath her and she tried to catch herself, imagining breaking at least two bones as she fell.

But thankfully, the cot was close enough to cushion her fall.

Before she could straighten herself, Cord Johnson had unlocked the cell door and rushed to her side.

"Are you all right, Doctor?"

Rebekah nodded as he helped her to her feet. She shook out her skirts to straighten them. "What are you doing here, Mr. Johnson? What's happening?"

He looked into her eyes and somehow managed to capture time and hold it still a moment.

What the reporter wrote was true indeed. Cord Johnson was able to stop time and hold it those precious moments a body needed to orient themselves. Or to die.

Cord said in his ever-soft-spoken tone, "We need you, Doc Beck."

CHAPTER 9

Getting arrested for the first time was one thing. Breaking out of jail was another matter entirely.

But Rebekah followed Cord Johnson right out the cell door, right past Deputy Bob who was hogged-tied and gagged in his chair and screeching through his throat, then right out the door to the quiet of Stark's Crossing.

Rebekah felt like her feet were made of wood as she clomped down the boardwalk beside Cord Johnson. At least he wasn't wearing his fringed leather jacket. But they were still an odd pair, especially with her wrinkled navy blue traveling suit that had seen time in jail.

Worse, coming out of the hotel restaurant just ahead were the two gossipy ladies who saw Rebekah earlier with Marshal Hastings.

Before Rebekah could think of what to do, Cord offered his arm and she quickly took it. He slowed to a casual stroll and tipped his hat with a tight smile at the two ladies, who looked between him and Rebekah with a scowl. They passed, whispering behind their hands.

Cord glanced back. "That was odd."

Rebekah kept her mouth shut.

They strolled down the boardwalk to the outskirts of town to a dry creek bed that led away from the buildings. After another glance over his shoulder, Cord broke into a run, holding Rebekah's arm with one hand and her waist with the other as they plunged into the darkness.

They skittered down the wall of the gully and through rocks and underbrush. They were a quarter of a mile out of town when the gully took a sharp turn. There was the wagon parked in the dry creek bed.

To Rebekah's horror, Ella was tied to a wagon wheel.

She was gagged and flailing, jerking against the strips of cloth that bound her wrists to the spokes, eyes wild under her hair, face streaked with tears.

Cord Johnson released Rebekah and knelt beside Ella. He put his hand on her arm, but she shrank away from him, still yanking against the ties.

Rebekah fumbled with the knotted cloth, trying to free Ella, but with each pull, Ella tightened them more.

"I need a knife," Rebekah said, desperately wishing she had her medical bag.

Cord put his hand over Rebekah's to stop her frantic attempt to untie the knots. "Doc Beck, I'm the one who tied her here."

Rebekah stared at him in disbelief, a shudder running through her. What had she been thinking, trusting this man?

But then she glanced at Ella who curled herself in a ball against the wagon, weeping. Then her body jerked and she leaned back, trying to use her body weight to break loose from the wheel.

A sinking feeling replaced the panic in the pit of Rebekah's stomach. Ella was in hysterics and Cord had secured her to keep her from hurting herself. If she ran away in the darkness, she could die in the wilderness before they found her. It was a mercy Ella was found near Defiant Plains and taken in.

"Mr. Johnson, we need to give her relief, now. Do you still have the chamomile?"

Cord shook his head. "I brewed her tea earlier but I couldn't get her to drink it. When she went into hysterics, I didn't know what else to do."

Rebekah looked around in the darkness, her mind scrambling for something that might help. She felt lost in this part of the country where the plants weren't as familiar and she didn't have her medical bag to rely on.

Ella gave a mighty jerk against the wagon wheel, pulling herself to her feet and raising her bound hands upward as though she could flip the wagon.

Cord rose, but didn't touch her as if afraid he would cause her more panic. He looked to Rebekah, eyes pooled with desperation, pleading for her to make his sister well. But Rebekah couldn't.

Understanding came into her soul with a suddenness that startled her. She whispered, "Then it's time."

It was time to put aside the sedation and bring Ella back to herself—if it was possible.

"It's going to be a long night, Mr. Johnson. We'll have to see her through and by morning, Lord willing, she'll regain her sanity."

CHAPTER 10

Going from the bunkhouse to Doc McKinnon's fancy study disoriented Jimmy every time. He took most of his reading lessons there with Miss Rebekah, but since this was his first time for Doc to take over, it made him jittery.

Doc McKinnon wasn't a stern man, but his demeanor and maturity was daunting for Jimmy as he tried to concentrate on the McGuffey Reader.

Doc McKinnon tapped the book, making the pages bounce. "Do we need to go over the alphabet more thoroughly, Jimmy? I didn't mean to get ahead of where Rebekah has you."

Jimmy sat up straight in the leather wing back chair where he was next to Doc McKinnon in front of the man's oak desk. Jimmy rested the McGuffey reader on his leg. He needed to stall for more time to make the letters line up into words to his eyes.

"I reckon I am thinking about her," he said. "You think she's all right? That telegram was pretty odd, like she might be in trouble or something."

Doc McKinnon leaned back, taking up his tea cup and saucer from the tall tea table between them. The coffee was cooled down from when Freddy the cook had looked in on them a half an hour ago and poured coffees.

Doc McKinnon took a sip and the corners of his eyes relaxed. But Jimmy could tell he'd given that telegram a lot of thought since it arrived earlier.

"Rebekah is often called to different places when she's doing her work," Doc said, his tone confident. "There's always a need for doctors that are spread so thin across the west. I'm sure she would have stated specifically if she needed help. She knows I would send Laramie Jones after her in a heartbeat."

Jimmy never could keep his emotions off his face and he knew his dedication for Miss Rebekah shone bright.

Doc McKinnon chuckled. "You too, of course, Jimmy. I don't discount the way you've stuck by her side since the two of you met."

Jimmy closed the book, ear marking the place with one finger. "Doc McKinnon, I'm pretty sure I've heard her call you 'uncle' a couple of times. Are y'all blood related? I mean, are you Omaha Indian, too?"

The man raised his eyebrows as he took another sip and Jimmy hoped he hadn't said anything wrong. He rushed on. "I know you're white, but you're kinda dark white."

Doc McKinnon chuckled. "Genetics are fickle, Jimmy, and you can't always judge a race by color. But no, I merely tan easily in this Wyoming sun."

Jimmy wasn't sure what genetics were, some kind of medical term, but he sure didn't want to judge anyone for anything.

Doc McKinnon paused, considering his next words. Doc always considered his words before speaking.

He seemed to make up his mind and said, "My sister was married to a missionary, John LaRoche, on the Omaha Indian Reservation. When John passed away, she chose to remain there. A few years later, she married Rebekah's widowed father, who had taken the LaRoche name years before in respect for the beloved missionary."

Jimmy felt like he'd been punched. "Miss Rebekah's last name ain't really hers? I mean, her pa got to pick his own last name and it got passed on to her?"

"That's right, Jimmy."

The shock wore off quick, leaving Jimmy awed by the notion that someone could pick their own last name for keeps.

Doc McKinnon went on. "Rebekah was a little girl when they married and knew I wasn't her blood relative, but we were family just the same. I love her like my own daughter. If I ever had a daughter."

Doc McKinnon stared at a spot on the front wall and Jimmy glanced back to see the row of black-and-white photographs on the bookcase.

Rebekah had come in on him staring at them one day and told him they were friends from Doc McKinnon's past. There was a pretty young woman and Rebekah said that was Bernadette Peterson, the woman from Hope Academy in New Mexico who Jimmy met when he snuck in with Miss Rebekah to help free those girls.

Doc McKinnon set his cup back on the table. "Let's see if we can't wrestle that page, Just Jimmy."

Jimmy quickly opened the book, willing his eyes to see straight. But the letters danced over the page, switching around every time he tried to pin them in one place. Still, he was determined to learn how to read after all the time Miss Rebekah had spent teaching him. She said he was a fast learner, but he didn't feel like it.

Doc McKinnon put his finger beneath one of the sentences, helping hold it still. "Now, we'll go over the phonetics of this word..."

The sound of horses trotting up the road to the house interrupted them. Doc McKinnon rose and went to the window, pulling back a lace curtain in the darkness of evening. It was past suppertime, well past time for anyone to pay a social call.

That was probably why Doc McKinnon frowned as he said over his shoulder, "It's Marshal Thorp from Centennial Ridge, along with a stranger."

Jimmy followed Doc McKinnon to the front foyer just as a knock sounded. Doc McKinnon opened it and Marshal Thorp stepped inside, taking off his hat and holding it in both hands. Jimmy knew the marshal from town, but when he saw the stranger, he exploded.

"You!" Jimmy hollered, balling his fist and getting ready to take a swing if the man said one wrong thing. "You're that reporter that did the story Miss Rebekah didn't like!"

The man grinned, sweeping off his derby hat and bowing to Jimmy. "What a fine young man you are, and what a fresh young memory you have."

To Doc McKinnon, he stuck out his hand to shake. "My name's Michael Hamilton, and this young fellow is right. I'm the scoundrel reporter who's always chasing down a good story. It's why I trailed the marshal here, though he cussed me every step of the way."

Jimmy didn't know Marshal Dave Thorp to have a foul mouth, but the lawman sure didn't look happy. Jimmy had a feeling it was the piece of paper he drew from his shirt pocket that had put a bur under his saddle.

"Sorry to bother you so late, Doc, but I've got bad news."

Doc McKinnon shook Hamilton's hand, though he never took his eyes off the marshal. Jimmy felt his own muscles brace up like Doc's as they got ready for the news.

"What's happened, Dave?" Doc asked.

Before the marshal could deliver his news, Laramie Jones came to the open front door. The foreman was aware of everything that went on at McKinnon Ranch.

Marshal Thorp glanced at Laramie, then flipped open the paper. Jimmy could tell it was a telegram.

The marshal hesitated, then said, "Doc Beck was arrested this afternoon."

Jimmy stared frozen, gape-mouthed. Laramie's eyebrows shot up as he snagged the telegram from Marshal Thorp.

The color drained from Doc McKinnon's face. "She was...what?"

"Hold on, Robert." The marshal rubbed his mouth. "That's not the bad news. She was broke out of jail this evening by Cord Johnson."

Doc McKinnon's expression changed instantly, though Jimmy didn't understand why. He did recognize the strain in Doc's voice as he echoed, "*The* Cord Johnson?"

Marshal Thorp sighed deep. "I'm afraid so."

The only sound in the foyer was Michael Hamilton's pencil scratching furious on his notepad.

Then Doc McKinnon snapped his attention to his ranch foreman. "Saddle my horse."

Jimmy wanted to bolt after Laramie Jones, get both of their horses saddled, but he couldn't move.

Marshal Thorp had more to say. "The deputy in Stark's Crossing said United States Marshal Hastings arrested her. But Hastings would never arrest a woman, not someone like Doc Beck. Something strange is going on there, Robert."

Jimmy scooted past Michael Hamilton to shoot out the door. Miss Rebekah was in trouble, sure enough.

CHAPTER 11

The night stretched longer and darker than Rebekah could have imagined. To keep Ella from harming herself, Rebekah decided to leave her bound, but removed the gag. Her screams ripped through the night and Rebekah allowed them as she stroked the woman's brow and spoke to her in soothing tones. When Rebekah's voice gave out, Cord filled in with stories of life on a Kansas farm with Ella.

During those long hours, Rebekah learned of their growing up years—hope when new animals were born, simplicity of daily chores, reading the Bible aloud in recent years.

For a quiet man, Cord never ran out of words to try and soothe his sister.

At last, deep in the night, Ella went limp. She tucked her head under her arm as she curled against the wheel.

Cord quietly retrieved two blankets from the wagon. He offered one to Rebekah, then draped the other over Ella, tucking it around her shoulders.

Rebekah wrapped herself in the blanket, beginning to feel the cold night air after breaking into a sweat while trying to comfort Ella.

Cord added wood to the dying fire. The pop of the dry wood catching fire startled Rebekah back to the reality of their situation. If anyone heard Ella's cries and Deputy Bob was hunting for the female doctor escapee, her time of freedom might be too short lived to see Ella back to sanity.

By the fire, Cord Johnson may have had the same thoughts as he remained crouched for action, staring into the darkness awhile. He was probably orienting himself to every noise and movement that lay beyond the circle of light.

Rebekah imagined even Marshal Hastings could have snuck up on him during those hours when his sole focus was on his sister, and Cord Johnson wouldn't have flinched from tending Ella.

Rebekah settled on the other side of the fire from him, knees drawn up and blanket wrapped around them. After all the distress, she should have enjoyed the quiet. But after what they just went through, she felt like she could ask Cord Johnson anything.

"How did you break out of jail back in Defiant Plains?"

Cord's expression remained unchanged. "I didn't break out. Marshal Wilde released me."

Rebekah cocked her head, raising an eyebrow in surprise. "But there was a warrant for your arrest."

Cord shifted to reach for another stick from the pile he'd collected. He tossed the dry stick in the fire, sending a spray of sparks skyward.

"There are no warrants out for me. The man calling himself Marshal Hastings lied."

Rebekah stared at Cord Johnson, prompting him to go on. He did.

"Marshal Hastings...he fits the description of Buck Callaghan, leader of the outlaws who kidnapped Ella."

Rebekah drew in a quick breath, recalling the way the marshal accosted and falsely arrested her. More so, she again experienced the feeling she had in Defiant Plains when she first met him and the instant distrust that came over her. If she had known he was Buck Callaghan, one of the most ruthless outlaws in the west, she would have gotten right back on that stage.

Cord closed his eyes, again reliving that day it seemed.

"He wore a bandanna over his face then, but his eyes...his hands. I'm almost certain he's the man who had Ella. The man who shot me."

Ella shifted, pushing one foot away from her, and Rebekah tensed. She felt Cord do the same. But when a soft snore rose from Ella, she let out a relieved sigh and turned back to Cord.

"Why didn't you tell me that first night you didn't break out of jail, that Marshal Wilde had no warrant for your arrest?"

Cord rubbed his hands together then spread them over the fire to warm them. He looked straight at her.

"Would you have believed me then, Doc Beck?"

Rebekah studied his face and those eyes that held her fast. The lines on his face told the story of his life—weathered and tanned skin from years of work on a farm, and the suppleness of a caretaking brother. Yet eyes still marked as a cool and calculating gunman.

There were so many layers to this simple-looking man that she didn't know how to answer his question. He was being honest in the moment; she suspected he had been every moment. She was, too.

"I cannot say for certain. But I do believe you now."

Cord returned his gaze to the darkness. Rebekah wondered how much he needed to watch the darkness within himself, knowing an enemy from his past could spring at him anytime.

"Will you go after Hastings once Ella is safe?"

"I never track down a man unless I'm certain he's guilty."

What he didn't add was, *track a man down to kill him,* but it was hanging there in the air. Cord Johnson had hunted down each man in the gang that kidnapped his sister. One by one. They were all dead, except their leader.

The question remained of whether Cord set out to kill them or that was simply a consequence of who he was. Rebekah supposed the answer lay within the inner darkness Cord Johnson battled. Was a gunman, who had killed for a living, truly redeemable?

There was no darkness when he was with his sister, that much was certain.

Maybe Cord and Ella Johnson could both return to that peace and redemption. The fact that Ella hadn't shown previous signs of mental instability gave Rebekah hope that perhaps the two could return to their farm in Cimarron, Kansas, and live happily ever after.

But was there really such a thing when their pasts scarred them so deeply?

Rebekah hoped so, as much as she hoped for it in her own life.

CHAPTER 12

An ear-piercing scream brought Rebekah instantly awake. She jerked upright and swept her hair away from her eyes, blinking against the brilliance of the morning sun. She'd been curled next to the fire, and remembered falling asleep there, Ella still tied to the wagon with cloths. The two women were the only ones in camp now, Rebekah gathering her senses while Ella screamed again as she fought the binds from her seated position.

Cord Johnson slid down into the gully, canteens in hand, water sloshing out of one of them from a missing cap. He had told Rebekah there was a spring nearby and he must have been off to fetch water when Ella awoke.

He reached her before Rebekah, dropping the canteens and letting water spill out. He wrapped his arms around Ella's shoulders as the woman breathed in great gasps.

Rebekah went to Ella's other side while Cord covered his sister's clenched hands with his, pressing his forehead against her matted hair.

"Please, please, remember me, Ella," he whispered. "I'm your brother. I will protect you. I love you."

His murmured words barely reached Rebekah. But before she could draw him away to examine Ella in the daylight, a thunderous sound echoed in Rebekah's ears.

Cord Johnson leaped to his feet, but not in time. Men on horseback broached three sides of the gully, guns drawn. Rebekah gasped, then saw Deputy Bob.

This was a posse hunting her down for escaping jail.

Rebekah wanted to laugh at how ridiculous the situation was. But the last rider coming into the gully sent a shiver of terror through her—the so-called Marshal Hastings.

Having jolted awake only minutes before by the scream that must have brought the posse, Rebekah quickly assessed the situation. Cord wasn't wearing his guns and Rebekah's pepperbox was tucked beneath her suit jacket that she used as a pillow near the fire. Too far away to help with Hastings aiming his six-gun at Cord Johnson. And her.

Hastings shouted, "Watch that man! He's a killer. He could kill three of us before anyone bats an eye."

His fear mongering, though justifiable, served to raise the tension of the twelve-man posse.

Deputy Bob licked his dusty lips. "He sure can. Got the drop on me quicker than a cat when he broke that lady out of jail. Not that she should've been in there maybe, but—"

"Shut up, Bob," Hastings growled. "This man's a killer and swore he'd never be taken alive."

Rebekah knew Hastings planned to get Cord Johnson killed right then if he could. He'd likely do the killing and claim Cord was going for his gun. And if he was really Buck Callaghan, Ella and Rebekah were as good as dead, too.

Since the posse's abrupt entrance, Cord hadn't moved, hands partly raised and spread open in surrender. But close to his side, with Ella trembling on the ground between them, Rebekah detected the pistol tucked in his belt. The one he promised to protect Ella with.

Ella buried her face in her arm and screamed again. The posse —average citizens of Stark's Crossing—stared wide-eyed at the deranged woman. Rebekah held up both hands as though she could stop bullets from flying in panic.

"I'm a doctor, and this woman needs my help. Please. I need to untie her from the wagon."

Hastings shouted, "It's a trick!"

Deputy Bob lowered his gun slightly. "That woman looks like she's in a bad way. Get her loose, Doc Beck."

Rebekah slowly knelt by Ella, cupping the woman's cheek and turning her face upward. Ella's eyes were glazed over, frightened, but Rebekah saw something else there. Hope?

Struggling with the tight knots, Rebekah wondered when the shooting would start. But she finally managed to free Ella and helped her to her feet.

Rebekah kept her back to the men as she positioned Ella in the direction she needed her to see. But Ella kept her eyes downcast, staring toward the fire.

Moving a step to the side, Rebekah whispered, "Ella, look at that man across from you. Do you know him?"

Ella swayed.

Hastings yelled, "He's got a gun in his belt!"

Rebekah grasped Ella's chin and tilted it up. "*Him*, Ella. Is that him?"

Ella's dull eyes snapped bright and her mouth opened in a silent scream. Rebekah glanced back to see Hastings swing his gun toward the women.

Ella screamed, "That's Buck Callaghan! Cord, get him!"

Rebekah felt a bullet whiz by her ear as she wrapped her arms around Ella's waist and swung her to the ground. They hit hard as the shooting continued.

One, two, three shots.

Then silence.

Rebekah rolled away from Ella to see Hastings—Buck

Callaghan—knocked from his horse and laid out on his back, dead from Cord Johnson's bullet. The other posse men stared dumbfounded at the speed and accuracy of the man they'd thought to arrest.

Cord flicked the smoking pistol to the ground and spread his hands wide again as he spoke to Deputy Bob.

"It's time we got all of this straightened out. Put away your weapons."

Deputy Bob hesitated, then motioned for the other men to holster their firearms as he did.

The tension punched out of the air, Cord knelt by the women. Rebekah scooted away, giving him room to lift Ella into his arms. Ella gasped, blinked, then stared him straight in the eyes with her matching ones.

"Cord. I knew you would come for me..."

She wrapped her arms around his shoulders and Cord hugged her close.

The sight of the brother and sister reunited at last brought tears in Rebekah's eyes, then she wept quietly. Cord raised his head and then opened one arm to pull her into the reunion.

If only this escapade didn't threaten to cost Rebekah her own sweet family reunion. But if it did, at least one family was whole again.

CHAPTER 13

A hot breakfast was just what the doctor ordered. Literally. Doctor McKinnon announced he was treating everyone to breakfast at the hotel restaurant, where they were now waiting for Rebekah and Ella.

Doctor McKinnon, Laramie Jones, Just Jimmy, and Michael Hamilton—of all people—had arrived in Stark's Crossing and were there when the posse returned with Rebekah and the Johnsons. It took a half an hour to sort things out with the town marshal, who finally arrived back in town and added a missing piece to the puzzle—the real Marshal Hastings was found murdered two weeks prior, over 100 miles from Defiant Plains.

At the hotel, Doctor McKinnon persuaded the manager to extend the breakfast serving time. He wanted to give Rebekah a few minutes to clean up and change into the fancy traveling outfit that was delivered to the hotel rooms Cord Johnson reserved for them the night before. They hadn't used those rooms after he spotted Marshal Hastings on the streets of Stark's Crossing.

Rebekah wouldn't mind a nap before breakfast, but the train returning to Centennial Ridge and McKinnon Ranch was due to pull out in an hour. She hurriedly brushed and pinned her hair the best she could, and started helping Ella with hers so they could be presentable for breakfast.

Ella was seated at the vanity, quiet, not having spoken to anyone except her brother. But there was peace in her eyes.

Rebekah pulled the woman's hair into a loose bun. Ella met Rebekah's eyes in the mirror.

"Thank you," she whispered.

Rebekah added the last pin and rested her hands on Ella's shoulders, giving them a squeeze of understanding. Just Jimmy once told her, *Nothing knits folks together like sweat and gun smoke.* He had an uncanny way of capturing truths.

Normal color was coming back into Ella's face, and Rebekah took that as a sign she was recovering well from the harsh sedative Buck Callaghan had told Marshal Wilde she was supposed to take.

Rebekah was grateful to be sending her off with Cord Johnson to their farm in Kansas rather than the asylum.

While Ella had many quiet evenings ahead in front of a fireplace with her brother to sort out her experience and heal, Rebekah knew she had an important question to ask before they parted.

She gave Ella's shoulders another squeeze. While she was a captive herself not so long ago, Rebekah didn't know exactly what the woman endured during her two months with the outlaw gang.

"Is there anything I can do for you, Miss Johnson? I am a physician, you know."

Ella shook her head and covered Rebekah's hand with her own.

"Thank you, Doc Beck, but no. They didn't harm me, not in body. I suppose I'm too much of an old maid." Her voice caught and she stared at her reflection in the mirror. "But it drove me mad to be with them, pillaging and killing as they ran wild through the territory. I held onto hope that Cord would find me. Then, one day, Buck Callaghan told me Cord was...that he was dead, that Buck had killed him in Cimarron. I went into hysterics and...I really cannot remember what happened beyond that. I suppose that is when Buck obtained the sedatives to keep me incapacitated. I don't even know how I got away from them. But thank God I did. Thank God, Cord is alive and found me. Thank God for you, Doc Beck."

A soft tap sounded at the hotel room door and Ella stiffened. Rebekah imagined it would take time before sudden noises stopped making her jump.

Judging by the soft tap, Rebekah had a feeling she knew who was on the other side. She opened the door.

Sure enough, Cord Johnson waited there, his blonde hair neatly combed. He was wearing the starched white shirt, tie, and trousers Rebekah had purchased for their incognito train ride. At least that money had gone to good use. He looked quite civilized, and every bit as handsome as in his buckskin jacket, though Rebekah hadn't been able to admit that to herself until now.

Cord nodded at Rebekah and glanced inside to his sister still seated at the vanity. "Are you ready for breakfast, Ella? Our train will be here in half an hour."

Ella closed her eyes and Rebekah could sense a shudder she understood go through her.

"I'm not hungry, Cord."

Rebekah knew her hesitation had less to do with hunger and more to do with having to face strangers after her exhausting ordeal.

Rebekah picked up the pillowcase containing her bundle of dirty clothes. "Mr. Johnson, why don't we have the hotel staff pack a breakfast for you and Ella? I'll ask them to hurry so you don't miss your train."

She opened the door wider, indicating for Cord to come in and stay with his sister.

Cord stepped in sideways, so that he was facing Rebekah. He

stared into her eyes for several moments and Rebekah gripped the doorknob.

Everything about his reputation was true. He was fast and deadly and could hold anyone frozen under the neutral but alert look in his eyes.

Then he blinked and dipped his head at her. "I'm grateful for everything you've done, Doc Beck. I would've lost Ella forever if not for you."

His hand reached toward Rebekah's. His fingers twitched, then he clenched them into a fist at his side. "I hope we see one another again someday."

Rebekah swallowed. "I would like that, Mr. Johnson. But I feel life will carry us in far different directions. I do truly hope the best for you and your sister, that you live long, peaceful lives on your farm."

Cord Johnson nodded and stepped aside for Rebekah to make her exit. She started around him, then hesitated.

Keeping her back to him, she whispered, "I do believe in complete redemption, Cord. You convinced me."

Holding the pillowcase close, she hurried out and down the hallway. She'd be grateful to collect her medical bag where it was waiting at the depot along with her missing carpetbag.

But mostly, she was grateful to escape Cord Johnson's presence before he drew her into his life again. He was a fine man. A truly redeemed man.

CHAPTER 14

In the hotel restaurant, a feast was spread at one of the large round tables that also held Doctor McKinnon, Jimmy, Laramie Jones, and Michael Hamilton. The reporter grinned as he stood with the other men upon Rebekah's entrance.

Laramie Jones pulled out a chair for her and she took it with a grateful sigh.

"I'm sorry for keeping you all waiting. I wanted to make sure Ella was ready for the train trip."

As everyone took their seats, Rebekah caught the attention of the waitress and ordered two breakfast sandwiches be wrapped up for the Johnsons.

When she finished, Michael Hamilton said, "You are always worth waiting on, Doc Beck. You make my job easy."

While Jimmy scowled at him, Rebekah chuckled but the heaviness in her chest subdued it.

"I always aim to please, Mr. Hamilton. But I fear the scandalous news of my arrest has already hit newspapers. It really couldn't have come at a worse time."

She met Doctor McKinnon's eyes and noted the worried look he tried to disguise. Their meeting with Senator Harris and the

Nebraskan governor was coming up and the last thing they needed were headlines reading, *Frontier Doctor Rebekah LaRoche arrested for aiding and abetting murderer's escape.*

As she heard Michael Hamilton say once, *"A lie can travel halfway around the world while the truth is still putting on its boots."*

Michael Hamilton dug into his plate of scrambled eggs, bacon, biscuits, pancakes, and toast. He was like her as a doctor—long spells between good meals.

But he paused before shoveling in his first bite to say, "Not to worry, Doc Beck. I've already got your story written and it'll outshine anything those wanna-be dime novelists publish. I'll see it goes through the AP wires to every newspaper in the country, of how you were falsely arrested and then cleared of all charges while saving an innocent woman's life. Trust me, you'll be the hero of the west when I get done."

A tingle of relief went through Rebekah. She so wanted to believe him, but only time would tell.

"I'm fairly certain you've already done that, Mr. Hamilton. But I would just as soon not be known at all."

They were halfway through their meal when Jimmy looked up with a start, then came to his feet, pulling his napkin out of his shirt collar. Rebekah looked over her shoulder to see what caught his and everyone's attention in the restaurant.

There, in the wide doorway of the hotel restaurant, was Cord Johnson and his sister Ella. He carried a small bag with their belongings, which must have included his double ivory handled six-guns. He wasn't wearing them. Cord's buckskin jacket was draped over his arm, Ella on his other arm as they came into the restaurant. Conversation slowly began again, though in whispers out of regard for the man filling the room with his reputation.

Cord guided Ella to Doctor McKinnon's table. "We wanted to say goodbye, and thank you for your help in straightening things out."

Doctor McKinnon nodded. "Hamilton will make certain

you're cleared in the newspapers as well. I think it's safe to say you can return your reputation as a gunfighter to the realms of legend, if you desire."

"I do."

Jimmy was still standing and Rebekah doubted he even realized it. Hamilton had likely awed him with stories of the famed gunfighter who had put away his guns when Jimmy was just an infant.

Jimmy nodded at Cord's jacket. "Mind if I touch it?"

Rebekah started to scold Jimmy for making the silly request, but Cord shook the buckskin jacket to the end of his arm and into his hand. He held it out to Jimmy.

"Maybe you'd like to have it. It's good for ranch work. Should've been all it was for."

Jimmy took the coat in both hands, reverently. "You really mean it, Mr. Johnson?"

Cord nodded. "I'm a farmer, nothing else. I'm eternally convinced."

His gaze drifted to Rebekah and lingered. Then he tipped his hat to everyone at the table. Cord and Ella Johnson strode out of the hotel—and out of Rebekah's life for good.

Doctor McKinnon asked Michael Hamilton about the Cord Johnson story he was writing, and conversation turned to other gunfighters Hamilton wrote about in the past.

From beside Rebekah, Laramie offered the gravy dish for her last biscuit and she took it. But he held on a second, causing her to look up and meet his eyes. He didn't hide his concern, a silent question asking if she was all right. If Cord Johnson had harmed her.

Rebekah blinked, thinking back over her escapade, from Cord Johnson holding up the stage to the shootout with Buck Callaghan.

She whispered, "I'm all right, Lee. Everything's all right."

Laramie shifted the bowl closer to her plate, allowing her to spoon gravy over her biscuit. He touched the back of her hand from behind the bowl, letting her know she didn't need to explain anything else. He understood. He always did, even without words.

Rebekah rested the spoon back in the bowl and took a deep breath before looking across the table at Doctor McKinnon. "I owe you an apology."

He raised one eyebrow. "Whatever for, my dear?"

Rebekah smiled, trying to appear sheepish and innocent. "You told me that whatever I did on this trip, to 'stay out of trouble.' I promise, really and truly, to do so from now on."

Doctor McKinnon chuckled, Michael Hamilton outright laughed, and Laramie and Jimmy joined in. Rebekah smiled. It was good to be with her people that she loved so much.

She met Laramie's eyes again, and admired how they were captivating in their own way.

Michael Hamilton, recovering from his laughter, asked, "How do you do it, Doc Beck? Keep giving me such good stories to write?"

Thoughts rippled through Rebekah's mind like the summer wind through prairie grass. She took hold of that wind.

"I suppose there are many reasons for the course of my life. Not the least of which is that I am of the upstream people. We go against the current."

That was what she must do to return home.

Dearest reader,

Thank you for reading *The Gunman (Doc Beck Westerns Book 7)*. I truly hope it entertained and delighted you!

If you fell in love with the main characters, Rebekah, aka "Doc Beck," and Jimmy, you'll be excited to know book 8, *Ape Man*, is available! You can order it on any major retail site or through www.SarahElisabethWrites.com.

I'd be thrilled if you took a moment to write your thoughts in the form of a review for *The Gunman* and post it on your favorite retail outlet and Goodreads. You'll help other readers find this series.

To discover more of my books, free short stories, and to generally stay in touch with me, I invite you to join my VIP reader newsletter. You'll receive a free copy of *The Executions*, book one in my *Choctaw Tribune* Historical Fiction series. Please join me through: bit.ly/ChoctawTribune.

Speaking of history, the character of Doc Beck was inspired by Dr. Susan La Flesche (Omaha), who is hailed as the first American Indian to earn a medical degree. In continued research, my mother found Dr. Isabel Cobb (Cherokee), the first woman physician in Indian Territory, in very nearly the same years as Dr. La Flesche.

Lastly, if you're not familiar with my heritage books based on my Choctaw history and culture, you can check them out on www.SarahElisabethWrites.com.

Questions? Send them my way: me@sarahelisabethwrites.com

—Sarah Elisabeth Sawyer
Historical Fiction and Western author
Tribal member of the Choctaw Nation of Oklahoma

CANYON WAR (DOC BECK WESTERNS BOOK 1)

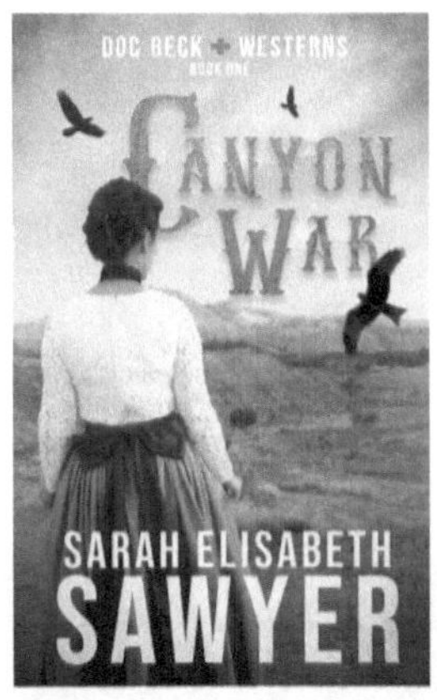

Traveling the West as a female physician, 34-year-old Doctor Rebekah LaRoche is no stranger to trouble. But on her way to New Mexico Territory, an unexpected stay in Amarillo, Texas, leads to confrontation with the Baxter clan – four brothers bred for trouble – and finds Rebekah in deep trouble.

Cattle rancher Clem Baxter's private war over grazing rights in the Palo Duro Canyon turns disastrous, and when the dust settles, one of the Baxter brothers is hurt bad. Clem sends for a doctor, not a woman, but that's what he gets when Rebekah, known as "Doc Beck," arrives at the ranch.

Now held at Clem's ranch against her will, Rebekah must plot to flee through the night with her young friend into the dangers and beauty of the Palo Duro Canyon.

Of Omaha Indian and French descent, Rebekah has always relied on her wits to get her out of any situation. But does that include facing down men willing to die—and kill—for a wild piece of land just as dangerous as any bullet?

***Canyon War* is available on multiple retailer sites.**

♦ ♦ ♦

MISSION BANDITS (DOC BECK WESTERNS BOOK 2)

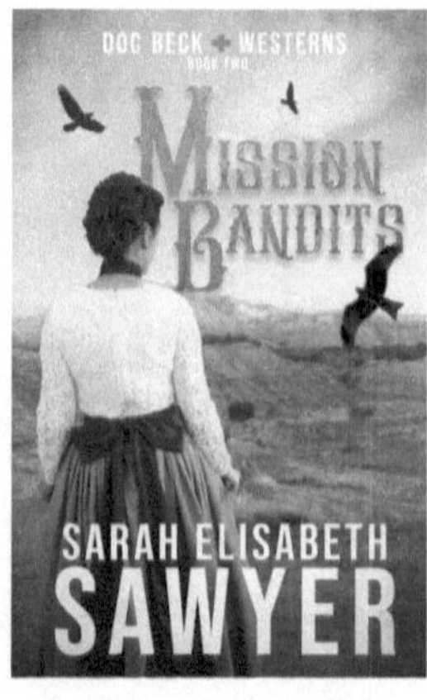

The Mexican army, a town marshal, and the Sancho Guerra gang are facing off when Doctor Rebekah LaRoche and her new friend, Jimmy, arrive in Zapata, New Mexico Territory. The bandits are holding hostages at Hope Academy, a school for girls located in an old mission outside of town, and Rebekah feels compelled to act—she was sent to the school to modernize the infirmary, not see the innocent occupants murdered.

The notorious and charismatic bandit, Sancho Guerra, led his band of men on a pillaging spree from Mexico to the mission and has proven his indifference to killing, prepared for any tricks the army or the Zapata town marshal throw at him.

But he isn't prepared for Rebekah, and now the Mexican army colonel wants her to do something terrifying—enter the mission and help with the capture of the deadliest men in the territory.

***Mission Bandits* is available on multiple retailer sites.**

GRAVE ROBBERS (DOC BECK WESTERNS BOOK 3)

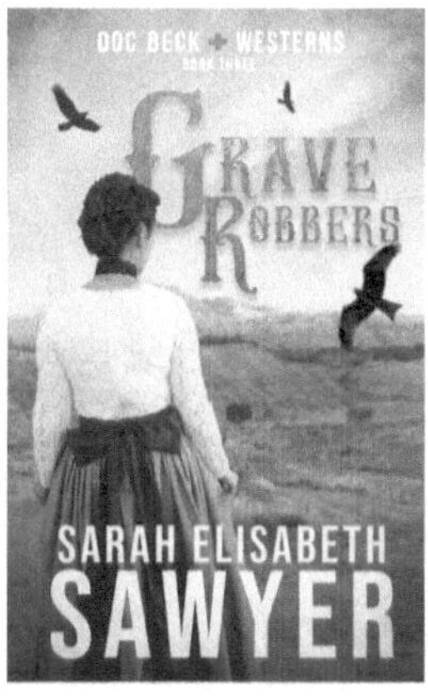

"You swing just as high for killing one as you do three."

Called on to perform an autopsy for a murder case, Doctor Rebekah LaRoche and Just Jimmy find themselves as unlikely detectives in a town with too many secrets.

One of the bandits who held the old mission and Rebekah hostage is accused of murdering Ruby Palmer, a young woman who took some of those secrets with her in death. When Rebekah discovers them during the autopsy, she must fight to prove her former captor is innocent. But she soon learns truth isn't something this town welcomes.

There isn't one straight shooter in the lot—the corrupt sheriff, judge, and leading townsmen are ready to lynch the bandit with hardly a trial. The only man Rebekah partly trusts is Deputy Thad Biggins. But what secret is driving him?

With the whole town against her, Rebekah finds herself at a crossroads: Let the bandit guilty of many crimes hang for one he didn't commit; or prove his innocence by robbing Ruby Palmer's grave.

Grave Robbers is available on multiple retailer sites.

DESERT CAPTIVE (DOC BECK WESTERNS BOOK 4)

If thou knewest the gift of God...thou wouldest have asked of him, and he would have given thee living water...

There comes a time when one questions every decision they've made in life. That moment is here for Doctor Rebekah LaRoche when she is taken captive by her nemesis, the bandit Sancho Guerra, and spirited across the desert to a hidden village in Mexico.

With no hope of rescue, Rebekah must earn a place among the families of bandits as a medical doctor until she can devise a way to reach the top of the road leading out of the valley—without being shot by the three sets of guards.

Little does Rebekah know that her long-time friend, Laramie Jones, is on his way to attempt a hopeless rescue. If she knew his plans, she'd beg him to stay away: no one has ever penetrated the bandits' valley and lived to tell about it.

With factions closing in all around her, time is ticking down toward an explosive conclusion, and Rebekah will have to draw on her greatest strength yet to survive.

***Desert Captive* is available on multiple retailer sites.**

◆◆◆

RANCH FEUD (DOC BECK WESTERNS BOOK 5)

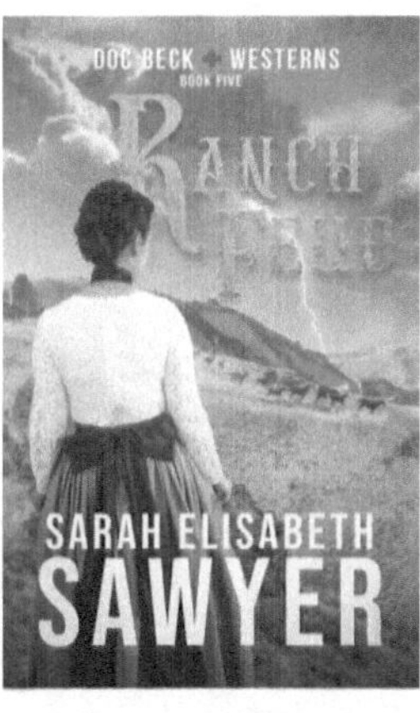

A feud dating back to the Civil War threatens Doc Beck's future...

Doctor Rebekah LaRoche is finally home in Wyoming—but trouble waits for her in spades, and a slim chance to return to the Omaha Indian Reservation grows slimmer when she's drawn into a feud between two powerful ranchers.

Glenn Butler and Dean Wallace hate each other's guts and have pitted their offspring against each other since birth. But it's Butler's daughter, Lilly, and her disgrace at law school that has Rebekah scrambling for answers. Rebekah wrote the letter of recommendation that helped Lilly be accepted into the college, and if she can't untangle the scandal and its connection to this powerful rivalry, she is doomed with another black mark on her professional reputation.

U.S. Senator Jeffrey Harris wants Rebekah to stay out of the young state's troubles if she hopes to have his help. But how can she stay out of something that's entangled her, threatening the last chance she has to return to her people?

Ranch Feud is available on multiple retailer sites.

◆ ◆ ◆

BRONC BUSTER (DOC BECK WESTERNS BOOK 6)

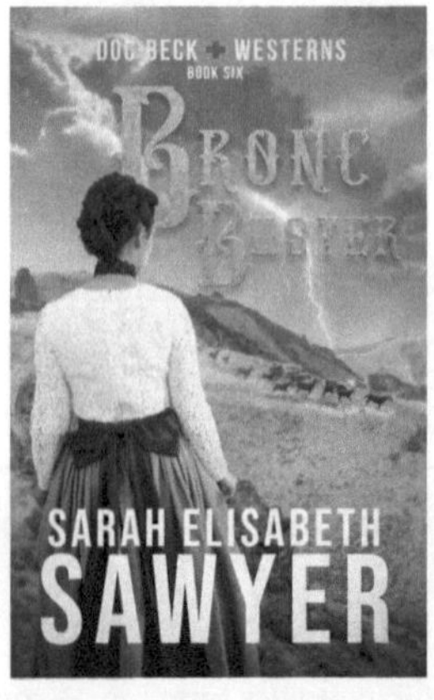

"Sometimes trail dust is thicker than blood."

There's nothing Just Jimmy wants more than to fit in with his new outfit on the McKinnon Ranch, and it's what Doctor Rebekah LaRoche needs, too—another piece in the puzzle of her returning to the Omaha Indian Reservation. But jealousy, a pressing contract with the U.S. Calvary, and soap soup quickly put Jimmy at odds with Steve Bowers, the new head wrangler.

Still shy of the horses they need and facing the looming contract deadline, Steve makes the bold suggestion to catch and break wild mustangs—except Jimmy and Steve aren't the only ones taking care of business in the rugged heart of the Medicine Bow Mountains.

When Jimmy stumbles upon orphaned triplets surviving off the mountain with their flock of sheep and trusty border collie, he must face not only their uncle's drunken rage and false accusation of rustling sheep —but a dark shadow from his own past.

Jimmy has a kind of wound Rebekah can't begin to heal until she understands what shaped the young man who has become her loyal companion. But are either of them prepared for a day when he will no longer be by her side?

Bronc Buster **is available on multiple retail sites.**

♦♦♦

APE MAN (DOC BECK WESTERNS BOOK 8)

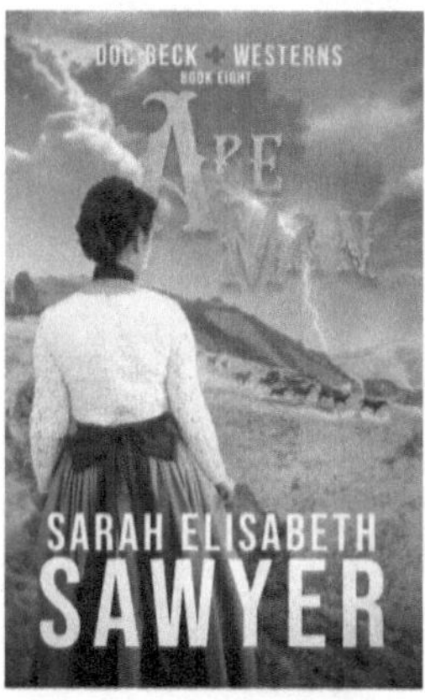

"He's dead."

When Doctor Rebekah LaRoche makes the pronouncement in Senator

Jeffrey Harris' office, her world is rocked by the death—and the note found beside the deceased. It's addressed to her personally: an ominous warning that those in her life always end up worse off because of her.

While the Donavan Brothers Circus rolls into Centennial Ridge, Wyoming, a murderous stalker tracks Rebekah's every move and targets those she loves. Death and near-death follow her in a terrifying sequence. But when Just Jimmy finds himself in the stalker's crosshairs, Rebekah unravels, ready to give up her quest to return home to the Omaha Indian Reservation for fear of endangering her relatives there.

Nowhere is truly safe for Rebekah as long as deadly secrets stalk her and tests of faith, regret, and forgiveness culminate in the Medicine Bow Mountains as a single terrifying fight for her own survival. "Doc Beck" has saved many lives—but can she save her own?

***Ape Man* is available on multiple retail sites.**

♦ ♦ ♦

THE EXECUTIONS (CHOCTAW TRIBUNE SERIES, BOOK 1)

Who would show up for their own execution?

It's 1892, Indian Territory. A war is brewing in the Choctaw Nation as two political parties fight out issues of old and new ways. Caught in the middle is eighteen-year-old Ruth Ann, a Choctaw who doesn't want to see her family killed.

In a small but booming pre-statehood town, her mixed blood family owns a controversial newspaper, the *Choctaw Tribune*. Ruth Ann wants to help spread the word about critical issues but there is danger for a female reporter on all fronts—socially, politically, even physically.

But what is truly worth dying for? This quest leads Ruth Ann and her brother Matthew, the stubborn editor of the fledgling *Choctaw Tribune*, to old Choctaw ways at the farm of a condemned murderer. It also brings them to head on clashes with leading townsmen who want their reports silenced no matter what.

More killings are ahead. Who will survive to know the truth? Will truth survive?

***The Executions* is available on multiple retailer sites.**

◆◆◆

TRAITORS (CHOCTAW TRIBUNE SERIES, BOOK 2)

"Nothing to it but a stout heart."

On a mission to bring justice to the outlaw gang that murdered his father and brother, Matthew Teller leaves the *Choctaw Tribune* newspaper for his sister to operate and plunges into an unfamiliar world of darkness and danger. Working inside the coal mines of the Choctaw Nation—one of the most dangerous places in the country—he searches for a man who may have the answers to this six-year-old mystery. But after Matthew uncovers an earth-shattering truth that rocks him to his core, he must decide what right is, and what price he is willing to pay for it.

Ruth Ann Teller knows she can handle publishing the *Choctaw Tribune*—until she loses their biggest advertiser. Now, with Matthew miles away and the future of the newspaper resting squarely on her shoulders, Ruth Ann must make a bold move to keep the newspaper afloat in her brother's absence. She sets it on a course for new success or total disaster.

Striking coal miners. Outlaw gangs. An unsolved crime. And a Choctaw family that fights for one another, and for truth.

Shaft of Truth (_Choctaw Tribune_ Series, Book 3) is available on multiple retailer sites.

◆◆◆

ANUMPA WARRIOR: CHOCTAW CODE TALKERS OF WORLD WAR I

The day I betrayed Isaac, I vowed never again to speak my native language in front of white men.

When America enters the Great War in 1917, Bertram Robert Dunn and his Choctaw buddies from Armstrong Academy join the army to protect their homes, their families, and their country. Hoping to find redemption for a horrible lie that betrayed his best friend, B.B. heads into the trenches of France—but what he discovers is a duty only his native tongue can fulfill.

War correspondent Matthew Teller is ready to quit until an encounter with a fellow Choctaw sets him on a path to write the untold story of

American Indian doughboys. But entrenched stereotypes and prejudices tear at his burning desire to spread truth.

With the Allies building toward the greatest offensive drive of the war, the American Expeditionary Forces face a superior enemy who intercepts their messages and knows their every move. Can the solution come from a people their own government stripped of culture and language?

Anumpa Warrior **is available on multiple retailer sites.**

TOUCH MY TEARS: TALES FROM THE TRAIL OF TEARS

For this collection of short stories, Choctaw authors from five U.S. states came together to present a part of their ancestors' journey, a way to honor those who walked the trail for their future. These stories not only capture a history and a culture, but the spirit, faith, and resilience of the Choctaw people.

Tears of sadness. Tears of joy. Touch and experience them.

Touch My Tears is available on multiple retailer sites.

◆ ◆ ◆

TUSHPA'S STORY (Touch My Tears Collection)

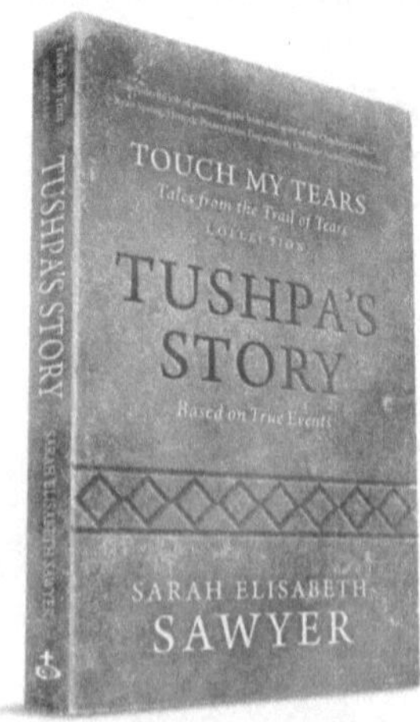

"Protect the book as you do our seed corn. We must have both to survive."

The Treaty of Dancing Rabbit Creek changed everything. The Choctaw Nation could no longer remain in their ancient homelands.

Young Tushpa, his family, and their small band embark on a trail of life and death. More death than life lay ahead.

On their journey to a new homeland, the faith of his father and one book guide Tushpa as he learns what it means to become a man and a leader.

But before long, betrayal from within and without rip at the unity of the band. Can Tushpa help keep his tattered people together? Or will they all be lost to sickness of the mind, body, and spirit on the four hundred mile walk?

A continuation of the anthology *Touch My Tears: Tales from the Trail of Tears*, this story follows an original manuscript written by Tushpa's son, James Culberson.

Tushpa's Story is available on multiple retailer sites.

ABOUT THE AUTHOR

SARAH ELISABETH SAWYER is a story archaeologist. She digs up shards of past lives, hopes, and truths, and pieces them together for readers today. The Smithsonian's National Museum of the American Indian honored her as a literary artist through their Artist Leadership Program for her work in preserving Choctaw Trail of Tears stories. A tribal member of the Choctaw Nation of Oklahoma, she writes historical fiction from her hometown in Texas, partnering with her mother, Lynda Kay Sawyer, in continued research for future works. Learn more at SarahElisabethWrites.com, Facebook.com/SarahElisabethSawyer